BODYGUARD

Book 2: Hostage

Also by Chris Bradford

The Bodyguard series
Book 1: Recruit
Book 2: Hostage
Book 3: Hijack
Book 4: Ransom

BODYGUARD

Book 2: Hostage

Chris Bradford

Philomel Books

PHILOMEL BOOKS
an imprint of Penguin Random House LLC
375 Hudson Street, New York, NY 10014

Copyright © 2014, 2017 by Chris Bradford.
First American edition published by Philomel Books in 2017. Adapted from
Hostage, originally published in the United Kingdom by Puffin Books in 2014.

Philomel Books is a registered trademark of Penguin Random House LLC.

Library of Congress Cataloging-in-Publication Data is available upon request.
Printed in the United States of America.
ISBN 9781524736996
10 9 8 7 6 5 4 3 2 1

American edition edited by Brian Geffen.
American edition design by Jennifer Chung.
Text set in 11-point Palatino Nova.

For Thomas and Benjamin,
two guardians in training!

"The best bodyguard is the one nobody notices."

With the rise of teen stars, the intense media focus on celebrity families and a new wave of millionaires and billionaires, adults are no longer the only target for hostage-taking, blackmail and assassination—kids are too.

That's why they need specialized protection ...

GUARDIAN

Guardian is a secret close-protection organization that differs from all other security outfits by training and supplying only young bodyguards.

Known as guardians, these highly skilled kids are more effective than the typical adult bodyguard, who can easily draw unwanted attention. Operating invisibly as a child's constant companion, a guardian provides the greatest possible protection for any high-profile or vulnerable young target.

In a life-threatening situation, a **guardian** is the final ring of defense.

PREVIOUSLY ON BODYGUARD . . .

Junior kickboxing champion Connor Reeves is recruited by a secret close-protection agency headed by the mysterious Colonel Black . . .

Connor laughed at the idea. "You can't be serious! I'm too young to be a bodyguard."

"That's *exactly* the point," replied a voice from behind him in a clipped military tone.

Connor spun around and was shocked to find the silver-haired man from the tournament standing right behind him.

"With training, you'll make the *perfect* bodyguard."

———

But during his training, Connor confronts the hard reality of failure as Charley Hunter, a fellow guardian severely injured on a mission, explains . . .

Charley glanced down at the badge. "These are awarded for outstanding bravery in the line of duty."

Intrigued, Connor asked, "What did you do?"

Charley rolled to a stop by the window and looked out at the mountains in the distance.

"As guardians, we hope for the best but plan for the worst," she said softly. "Sometimes, the worst happens."

———

And in this increasingly dangerous world, the worst does happen: Malik Hussain, leader of a Middle Eastern terrorist group, declares war on the United States . . .

"We must hit America where it hurts the most," he continued, his fervor building. "A wise man once said, 'Kill a few, hurt many, scare thousands.' But in this attack, we need only kidnap *one* infidel."

He paused, relishing the moment of power as his men leaned in, mesmerized by his words.

"Who's the target?" breathed Bahir.

"The president's daughter."

———

Fortunately President Mendez is taking necessary, if somewhat unusual, precautions for his daughter's safety . . .

"Contact Colonel Black immediately," he instructed. "Tell him that we'll be requiring his organization's services."

Dirk leaped from the sofa to look at the profile in George's grasp. As he scanned the president's choice, his expression crumbled into one of sheer disbelief. "But this guardian hasn't even completed a single assignment yet!"

The president closed the file and replied with complete conviction. "He's the one."

———— ————

On hearing of his assignment, Connor is equally bewildered by the president's decision until . . .

No longer able to contain the burning question that had been on his mind ever since his selection, Connor put down his undrunk cup of coffee and asked, "Why did you choose *me*?"

President Mendez clasped his hands almost as if in prayer. "I would have thought that was obvious. Your father saved my life."

———— ————

However, Alicia Mendez doesn't want to be guarded. She just wants to have fun. With no clue that Connor is her bodyguard, she tries to evade the Secret Service and lead him astray . . .

"Wait!" cried Connor, realizing now why Alicia was the captain of her school track team.

He pursued her down a deserted side street. But Alicia was still pulling away.

"Keep up!" she called, giggling at the thrill of her escape.

Grateful for all his fitness training, Connor put on a burst of speed. His sneakers pounded the concrete as he followed her left onto the main road. Then lost her . . .

——— ———

Alicia's actions play straight into the terrorists' hands . . .

"Eagle Chick has flown the nest!"

Malik stopped sharpening his *jambiya* and smirked to himself. "It's almost as if she *wants* to be taken hostage."

The phone buzzed again and Bahir read the message out loud. "It's from Hazim—*Sparrows in a panic*. It appears the Secret Service agents are having trouble locating her!" he laughed. Bahir turned excitedly to his leader. "*This* could be our chance."

——— ———

Putting both Connor and Alicia directly into the path of mortal danger . . .

"Behind you!" cried Alicia as Crew Cut now charged in.

Connor spun to face the other gang member. In Crew Cut's hand flashed the ominous steel glint of a switchblade. Alicia screamed as she saw the knife plunge into Connor's side . . .

1

Connor felt a sharp stab of pain in his ribs as the blade hit its mark . . .

But the adrenaline blocked the rest of the damage.

Battling for his own survival as well as Alicia's, Connor fought with the fury of a tiger. He palm-struck Crew Cut in the face, stunning and weakening his opponent. Then, grabbing the gang member's hand that held the knife, he spun himself under Crew Cut's arm. The whole series of joints from wrist to shoulder twisted against themselves. The effect was instantly crippling. Crew Cut's elbow hyperextended until it snapped out of joint with a sickening pop. Crew Cut bawled in agony and dropped the switchblade. Kicking the knife away, Connor then finished off the gang member with a strike to a pressure point at the back of his skull. Crew Cut ceased screaming and crumpled to the ground.

After ensuring there were no other immediate threats, Connor pulled Alicia to her feet.

"Are you hurt?" he asked.

"Me?" gasped Alicia, panting from the shock of the attack. "I should be asking *you*."

"I'm fine."

"But I could have sworn he stabbed you."

Lifting his black T-shirt, Connor inspected his ribs. There was a small round bruise forming, but the knife hadn't penetrated his skin. He thanked his lucky stars for the stab-proof T-shirt Jody had given him.

"Just missed me," he said, quickly lowering his shirt so she didn't question his miraculous survival.

They turned their attention to the two gang members who lay unconscious on the road.

"I can't believe it," said Alicia, studying Connor in a new light. "Where did you learn to fight like that?"

"I've trained a bit in kickboxing," he admitted.

Alicia gave an astonished laugh. "A bit? You're more deadly than the Secret Service!"

"Look, we have to get out of here," replied Connor. "There may be others."

Hurriedly gathering the contents of Alicia's bag, including his phone, he noticed the panic alarm was already clasped in her hand. So *that* was why she'd been so determined to retrieve her belongings.

As they turned to go, Connor noticed a huge bearded man heading toward them, then three black limos screeched to a halt at the end of the alley. In a matter of seconds Secret Service agents had piled out, guns at the ready. Taking one look at the agents bristling with weapons, the bearded man fled. They cordoned off the area, three of them immediately surrounding Alicia. Two others began inspecting the comatose gang members and handcuffing them.

"What happened?" demanded Kyle, his eyes sweeping the alley for further danger.

"We were mugged," explained Connor.

"I can see that. I mean . . . back at the clothing store." He glared at Connor, clearly wanting to say more. But he held his tongue, realizing he couldn't blow Connor's cover.

"It's my fault, Kyle," said Alicia boldly. "I wanted a little adventure. On my own."

"Well, you certainly got it," he replied, struggling to maintain his professional composure. "You could have been *seriously* hurt."

Alicia shook her head. "Not with my knight in shining armor by my side," she replied.

Smiling, she took Connor's arm and strode off toward the waiting limo.

2

"What were you trying to prove?" Dirk demanded, his steel-blue eyes boring into Connor. "That you're some sort of hero?"

"I was just doing my job," replied Connor, sitting on the opposite side of the conference table in the Roosevelt Room. As soon as they'd returned to the White House, he'd been summoned to the West Wing by the director of the Secret Service for a crisis meeting. Kyle had already been grilled by the director, and now it was his turn.

"Your 'job' is to inform the Secret Service *immediately* of her intentions."

"I'd have broken Alicia's trust if I'd done that."

Dirk gave a hollow laugh. "Trust is the last thing you should be concerned about. Your very presence is a deception."

"That wasn't my choice," replied Connor, shifting uncomfortably in his seat. "But, if Alicia's going to run away, isn't it better if I'm with her?"

"Not if you introduce her to city gangs!" he snapped, hammering the mahogany table with his fist. "You put Alicia's life at great risk, boy. As you well know, your appointment was against my better judgment. And I've been proved right. You're a tragedy waiting to happen, Connor Reeves."

Before Connor had a chance to defend himself, there was a knock at the door and the president's secretary popped her head around.

"Dirk, the president will see you now."

The director of the Secret Service shot Connor a withering look. "I hope you've got a thick skin, because you're about to be flayed alive."

Connor swallowed nervously. He thought he'd done the right thing. And he *had* protected Alicia when it mattered most. But now he questioned his judgment. Even he realized that they could have avoided trouble if he'd just warned Kyle. But it was too late to change that. He had to live with his decisions. Bracing himself to be sent home in shame, Connor followed the director and Kyle into the Oval Office. President Mendez was standing by the window, his back to them. The White House chief of staff, George Taylor, was also present. He greeted them with a strained smile.

"So what happened?" asked President Mendez, his expression grave as he faced them.

Dirk stepped forward and gave his report. "First and foremost, your daughter is safe and unharmed," he began, before proceeding to deliver an account that was more or less accurate, although Connor's actions were not presented in a favorable light. "So you see, Connor's lack of communication and disregard for protocol resulted in your daughter being placed unnecessarily in harm's way. Fortunately, as soon as the panic alarm was triggered, my Secret Service team secured her safety," Dirk concluded.

"Why couldn't you just track Alicia's position like the last time?" asked George.

"She switched off her cell phone," explained Kyle. "Alicia's gotten wise to our tricks."

"Short of implanting a GPS tracker, there's not much we can do about that," Dirk said. "The panic alarm pinpoints her position, but only when *she* triggers it."

President Mendez frowned and sighed. "I see your point. And she certainly won't accept any further invasion of her privacy. Once again I must apologize for my daughter's wayward nature. Like her mother, she needs her freedom. But there's one matter I need to have clarified. Who actually tackled the two gang members?"

Dirk was slow to answer, clearly reluctant to give Connor any credit. But Kyle spoke up.

"The two threats were eliminated *before* our arrival, Mr. President," he replied. "By Connor, in fact."

Connor looked over at Kyle in surprise. He hadn't expected the agent to back him up, especially with his boss present.

Nor apparently had Dirk, whose jaw fell open in disbelief.

President Mendez gave a satisfied nod, as if he'd almost expected that answer. Striding over to Connor, he laid a hand on his shoulder. "Well, Connor, you've certainly lived up to my expectations. I knew I could trust a Reeves bodyguard. Keep up the good work."

"Aren't we all missing the point here?" interjected Dirk. "We were lucky this time, but we can't risk this happening again. *Ever.*"

"Perhaps the shock of the mugging will convince Alicia of the necessity for the Secret Service," suggested George. "Maybe she won't be so eager to fly the nest now."

"I sincerely hope so," Dirk replied. "But we can't guarantee it. And we can't have *anyone* on the team going along with her escapades."

The director stared at Connor, making it known that he blamed him for the fiasco.

"But, Dirk, this is precisely the reason we hired Connor in the first place. He should be congratulated, not criticized," said President Mendez. He held up his hand to prevent any further protests from the director. "Let me have *another* word with Alicia. And ideally this will be the end of it."

With a weary shake of his head, he walked back to the window and gazed out at the Rose Garden. "Sometimes, I think bringing up a teenage daughter is harder than governing the country."

3

Ensuring he was alone in the rear kitchen, Malik switched on the untraceable cell phone he'd acquired from his contact. Then he dialed the number he'd committed to memory. It was answered on the fourth ring, and there was a burst of high-pitched squealing and electronic chatter as the scrambled signals synchronized with one another.

A digitally enhanced robotic voice spoke. *"Answer?"*

"All war is deception," replied Malik, quoting the Chinese philosopher Sun Tzu, as dictated by his contact instructions.

"Proceed with your update."

Malik had no idea of the identity of the person on the other end. Nor did he ever want to know. Anonymity was critical for the isolation of each cell—and even more so for the central cell. *They* had contacted him first. *They* had proposed the plan. And *they* had given him the means to carry it out. But *he* would be the one to receive all the glory.

He would be seen as the leading light. And the rest of the Brotherhood need never know of their existence or the part the central cell had played. That had been the deal.

"Eagle Chick unexpectedly flew the nest," Malik reported. "We almost had her in our net. But the sparrows flocked before we could grab her."

"What about your plan to clip Eagle Chick's wings while on the move?"

Malik had put a great deal of time, effort and resources into snatching the president's daughter on her school run. But the severely restricted time window, the presence of so many armed agents and the rush-hour traffic had presented too high a casualty risk for his men and hampered their chances of making a clean escape.

"I have a better, bolder plan," he replied.

"When will this new *plan be ready to execute?"* The contact's voice sounded irritated.

"The egg is about to be laid in the nest. It'll be ready to hatch in a couple of days," Malik replied confidently. "All units are set to go."

There was a pause on the end of the line.

"Has the operation been compromised in any way?" asked the robotic voice.

"No," said Malik with absolute certainty. "The sleeper has not awakened."

"Then execute operation without delay."

Malik's hand holding the phone began to tremble in anticipation. The time had come to make history.

"One question," he said, sensing the receiver about to hang up. "My final payment?"

Another pause. *"When the operation succeeds, you'll be* justly *rewarded."*

Malik grinned at the thought.

"Is that all?" said the voice, a trace of impatience detectable in its manipulated tone.

"Yes."

"Then this will be our last communication."

4

That evening Connor pounded the punching bag in the White House gym. Now that the adrenaline rush from the attack had faded, the harsh reality of what had happened hit home. Only in hindsight did he realize how close he'd come to serious injury and even death. He may well have dealt with both gangsters and protected Alicia, but he'd still been stabbed in the process. And he found himself agreeing with the director of the Secret Service—next time he might not be so lucky or be wearing his stab-proof shirt.

That thought made him train harder. He pummeled the bag. *Jab, cross, jab, hook!* His hands began to tremble under the effort. But he had to ensure his combat skills were up to scratch. From now on, he vowed to do extra martial arts training every morning. Not just for his own safety, but for Alicia's too.

His phone rang. Pulling off his gloves, he picked it up and saw the Guardian logo flashing for a video call. He pressed his thumb to the screen, and Charley's concerned face appeared.

"Are you all right, Connor? You missed your report time," she said.

"Just overshot on my training, that's all," he replied, wiping the perspiration from his brow with a towel.

Charley saw straight through his attempt at bravado. "I know what happened, Connor. The Secret Service got in contact when they were trying to locate you and Alicia. Next time, don't switch off your phone. I can't find you otherwise."

Hearing the edge of concern in her voice, Connor said, "Sorry—my fault. I made some serious mistakes today."

He sat down on the weight bench and retold his version of the events: his decision to follow Alicia and not to inform the Secret Service, allowing her to take his phone and switch it off, his stupidity in forgetting the second gangster, and his failure to defend himself properly.

"Don't be so hard on yourself," said Charley, trying to comfort him with a smile. "You should be proud of what you achieved. The bottom line is Alicia's alive and unharmed thanks to your quick reactions. And Colonel Black issues body armor precisely for those moments when we're overwhelmed or taken by surprise."

Connor felt better hearing this from Charley. Since she was the most experienced member of the team, he valued her opinion. He decided to bring up the other issue that had been gnawing away at him since the start of the operation.

"I'm getting to like Alicia," he admitted, then saw Charley's lips tighten in disapproval. "As a friend," he hastened to add. "Which is why I'm finding it hard not to let her know who I really am."

"It's for her own safety, Connor," Charley reminded him. "You've just proved today how valuable your presence is."

"But doesn't that go against the very principles of being a bodyguard? Colonel Black's always stressing how important integrity and honesty are to our job."

"Yes, it does," said Charley. "But sometimes because of the nature of an operation, a guardian has to remain covert—even to their Principal. Your role is to protect Alicia, but it is the president who is our client. We're required to comply with his instructions, and that means concealing your true purpose."

"But I can't hang around Alicia forever without her eventually suspecting something."

"Colonel Black's well aware of that possibility," Charley replied. "And we'll have to cross that bridge when we come to it. In the meantime, stay on guard. I fear there may be a storm coming."

Connor sat up straight. "Have you intercepted more threats?"

"No, exactly the opposite. It's gone quiet."

5

"They literally came out of *nowhere*," revealed Alicia to her friends, who sat transfixed on a picnic bench in the school-yard. "One moment we were walking to the park; the next these two guys jumped us."

Not exactly out of nowhere, thought Connor, recalling their carefully planned assault.

"I bet that was terrifying," said Kalila.

"It sure was!" Alicia replied. "But Connor wasn't scared. He leaped straight into action, even though one of them had a *knife*."

The girls all gazed at Connor in awe.

"You're *so* brave," remarked Paige.

"It was nothing," replied Connor, wishing to downplay his role. "Anyone in my shoes would have done the same."

"No, they wouldn't," protested Alicia. "Connor, you took them *both* down in seconds. You were truly amazing!"

"Serves them right too," said Grace.

"But where were the Secret Service agents?" asked Kalila.

Alicia offered a guilty smile. "We ditched them."

"Yeah, but who needs the Secret Service when you've got Connor!" Grace said, laughing as she struck a fighting pose. "He's a ninja warrior!"

Nudging Kalila, Paige whispered, "If I didn't already have a date for the dance, I know who I'd want to take me."

"Hands off, Paige, he's mine!" said Grace, putting a possessive arm around Connor's shoulders.

Alicia gently pushed her friend away. "Hey, you're already going with Darryl."

"Darryl *who?*" replied Grace innocently, and the girls laughed.

Although flattered by the attention, Connor hoped it would soon die down. If any of the girls actually *did* have a crush on him, it might compromise his ability to protect Alicia. There was even the risk that one of them might guess his true role.

As the girls pressed Alicia for more details of Connor's heroism, Connor glanced at his new watch—a gift from the president for protecting his daughter. He'd felt awkward about accepting it, but the president had insisted. Surprisingly, Dirk Moran had also encouraged him to accept it, afterward instructing Connor to wear it night and day. It was then that Connor discovered from Amir that the watch had been implanted with a micro-GPS tracker by the director. The

Secret Service had also been granted access to his smart-phone locator. Dirk was taking no more chances with him—wherever he went, the Secret Service would know.

"Now I wish I'd come along," said Paige. "It sounds so exciting."

"Next time I'll call you so you don't miss any of the action," joked Alicia.

"That reminds me," said Kalila, rummaging through her bag. "My eldest brother bought me a new phone."

"Lucky you!" said Grace. "The most my brother's ever given me is his old laptop."

Kalila pulled out a slim touch-screen phone. "I'd better give you my new number."

The girls bumped phones and transferred contact details.

"What about Connor?" Paige suggested. "You never know when you might need his protection."

"Well . . . okay," said Kalila, turning shy at the idea. "But if you do call me, Connor, I'll have to put your number under a girl's name, just in case any of my brothers happen to see."

"No problem," said Connor, unlocking his phone. "You can put me in as Daisy if you want."

Giggling at the suggestion, Kalila bumped phones and Connor accepted the incoming contact card containing her details.

"So this is where the tough guy hangs out?" said Ethan, swaggering over to their picnic bench. "With the girls!"

Behind Ethan, Jimbo glared at Connor, doing his best to intimidate him. Connor groaned inwardly at their appearance. Clearly, word of Alicia's mugging was spreading through the school like wildfire.

"Not jealous, are we?" goaded Grace.

Ethan snorted. "Me? He only beat up a couple of street bums. I've hit more home runs this season than any batter in the state. There's no contest!"

"But Connor saved Alicia's life," said Kalila.

"Well, if *I'd* been with Alicia, those bums wouldn't have gotten within spitting distance in the first place." He turned to Alicia and puffed out his chest. "Next time you want to go out in DC, stick with me."

Connor couldn't believe the boy's arrogance. And he very much doubted whether Ethan would have even noticed the muggers approaching, let alone have had the courage to stand and fight.

"Speaking of which, Alicia," continued Ethan, "have you come to a decision yet?"

"About what?"

"The school dance!" he cried in exasperation.

Alicia looked thoroughly unimpressed by his second clumsy attempt at asking her.

"Sorry," she replied, and faked an apologetic smile. "I'm already going with someone else."

Connor glanced over in surprise. This was news to him.

And judging by the reaction of her friends, news to them too.

"*What?*" exclaimed Ethan, disbelief written all over his face.

Alicia looped her arm through Connor's. "My knight in shining armor is taking me."

6

Hazim sat on the edge of his bed, the Glock 17 cradled in his lap.

The handgun was light, less than two pounds fully-loaded. But the weapon weighed heavy on his conscience.

He recalled how the soldiers had fallen under the storm of bullets from the submachine gunfire at the shooting range. How the target of a woman had spun and juddered as he'd winged her with a couple of shots. How a red haze had descended over him. Then how he'd literally *shredded* the little girl with the teddy bear in her arms before managing to release the trigger.

At the time it had all seemed like a harmless carnival game, with no real casualties. But now the truth confronted him in all its hard simple clarity, the reality as blunt as the bullets he'd just loaded into the gun.

It wouldn't be cardboard targets that were hit with these lethal rounds.

It would be flesh and blood.

People would die.

Children.

How could God condone such acts?

Whether an infidel or not, they were all human. Didn't the holy text say that the slaying of one human life was the same as slaying all mankind?

Yet his uncle had argued that non-believers were *not* the same. That disbelief was worse than killing and therefore the killing of non-believers justified. So infidels didn't warrant the same holy protection as those of the Faith.

And when it came to testing his own faith, could he kill in the name of God?

Hazim knew his faith was strong. But was it strong enough for the struggle ahead?

7

All eyes turned toward Connor and Alicia as they made their entrance into the school dance. Montarose was a very fancy private school, so naturally this was a very fancy affair. It was certainly the first time Connor had worn a tuxedo and black bow tie, and he was enjoying the James Bond look. It seemed appropriate for a bodyguard. Next to him, Alicia looked truly stunning in a flowing red silk dress, her long dark hair adorned with a cascade of miniature roses. And Connor couldn't help feeling a sense of pride as he walked across the school gym with the president's daughter on his arm.

The gym had been transformed into a glittering ballroom, festooned with purple and white streamers, flashing spotlights, lasers and a huge disco ball that dazzled like a diamond in the center of the room. Onstage a live band was playing, and the dance floor was already abuzz with students celebrating the end of the school year. Around the edge, tables were laden with food for a buffet.

"You look gorgeous," gushed Paige, welcoming Alicia and Connor to their table.

"So do you," replied Alicia. She stepped back to admire her friend's champagne-colored gown.

"This is Carl," said Paige, introducing her date, a tall handsome boy with cropped black hair and a chiseled jaw. "He's from Sidwell Friends School."

Alicia smiled warmly. "So *you're* the Carl that Paige has been hiding from us."

"Must be," he replied with a laugh. "Unless she's hiding some others."

Paige playfully bashed him on the arm with her purse. Then she leaned close to Alicia's ear and with an impish grin revealed, "Carl's two years older than us!"

Alicia raised an eyebrow in both surprise and approval.

Connor nodded to the older boy and introduced himself. Carl was just one of many new faces in the hall, the dance being open to student guests. This fact in itself presented an additional security problem for the Secret Service, especially since the school principal had deemed it inappropriate to search attendees on arrival.

Already seated around the table were Grace and Darryl, a laid-back boy from their year whose father was the Barbados ambassador. He raised his hand in acknowledgment of

Connor while Grace hugged Alicia. Kalila sat next to them with her date—another face Connor didn't recognize—an older boy with sleepy eyes and a sour expression suggesting he didn't want to be there at all.

As Alicia and Kalila kissed cheeks, Connor heard them whisper.

"So who's your date?" asked Alicia.

"Fariq," Kalila replied. "A friend of the family and the *only* one my father would approve."

Connor went over to say hello, but after a few attempts at conversation, he gave up with the monosyllabic guest. Connor pitied Kalila. She deserved a better date than this bore.

The band began belting out a hit by teen rock star Ash Wild, and more students joined the party.

"Come on, let's dance!" suggested Grace, grabbing hold of Darryl's hand.

As Darryl was dragged somewhat unwillingly from his chair, Carl and Paige rose to join them. Alicia turned expectantly to Connor.

"Are you sure you want to risk it again?" said Connor.

"Don't worry, I can handle a little danger," she assured him with a toying smile. "And I *know* you can."

"Okay," agreed Connor. "But be prepared to take your feet to the hospital!"

Alicia glanced over at Kalila and her date. "How about you two?"

Fariq seemed decidedly uncomfortable with the idea.

"Maybe later," said Kalila, offering a strained smile.

Reluctantly leaving them alone at the table, Connor and Alicia made their way over to the others on the dance floor. The music was pumping, and everyone was jumping to the beat. Alicia immediately got into the rhythm, her flowing movements making her appear as though she were dancing on air. By comparison, Connor appeared awkwardly stilted, but as soon as Alicia took his hand and reminded him of some of the salsa steps, his movement became more natural.

"That's more like it," Alicia said, beaming. She stepped away and began to lose herself in the music.

Dancing alongside Alicia, Connor momentarily forgot his role as a bodyguard and began to properly enjoy himself for the first time since arriving in the United States. He hadn't fully appreciated how stressful the past two weeks of covert protection had been. There hadn't been a single moment in Alicia's presence when he hadn't been thinking of her safety. That constant alertness eventually took its toll. So, all things considered, he felt he deserved a short break. Besides, after preventing the attempted mugging by the two gangsters, he was feeling more confident in his role. He'd proved he was up to the task.

As the dance floor grew more crowded, Connor's enjoyment was rudely interrupted by a sharp elbow in the ribs. Then another. Harder this time. Cursing himself for being in a state of Code White, Connor turned around to discover Ethan right behind him.

"Sorry," said Ethan harshly. "I didn't see you."

Connor doubted that, especially when a few moments later he was knocked into again.

"Watch it!" Ethan snarled as if it had been Connor's fault this time.

Realizing the boy was trying to goad him into a fight, Connor moved away. But he was bumped into from the other side by the mass bulk of Jimbo. Blocked in, Connor was unable to avoid Ethan's fist, disguised as a bad dance move. It struck him in the kidneys, and he almost buckled under the blow.

"Are you all right?" asked Alicia, suddenly noticing Connor's pained expression.

Ethan and Jimbo had danced away into the crowd.

"Fine," he replied through gritted teeth.

But, as soon as Alicia turned away, Ethan and Jimbo moved in for another attack. Connor didn't want this to escalate into a full-blown fight. That was a sure way to get thrown out of the school dance, embarrass Alicia and, most importantly, prevent him from protecting her.

But he had to end their bullying tactics. There and then.

Still appearing to dance, Connor spun on the spot, stepped on Ethan's toes, then drove his shin into his attacker's lower leg. Pushing against the joint, Ethan's knee locked up and, with Connor's foot pinning his toes to the ground, Ethan lost all balance. Connor's subtle jujitsu attack went unseen. But Ethan went sprawling across the dance floor in full view of everyone.

"What's he doing?" asked Alicia as the school's baseball star took out two dancers and Jimbo on the way down.

"Not sure," replied Connor, edging them away from the scene. "I *think* he was attempting to break-dance."

8

"I'm FREE to do what I WANT!" Alicia sang along to the band's music as she pirouetted on the dance floor.

Connor grinned at her gleeful performance. She'd hardly stopped dancing all night, only pausing for the buffet. With no Secret Service agents permitted within the gym itself, Alicia had felt able to spread her wings and truly let go. Connor knew Kyle and his protection team were standing guard around the school grounds, securing the perimeter. But there was no one *directly* looking over her shoulder—that she knew of, at least.

After the previous incident, President Mendez had requested that the Secret Service give his daughter more freedom. In return, Alicia promised not to run off again. Dirk Moran wasn't convinced about the idea of relaxing security arrangements. But the president had argued that Connor's presence meant there was less need for agents close by, especially during social engagements like the school dance.

The director had finally submitted to the president's will with the proviso that Connor wear his covert earpiece. With so many nonvetted guests attending the dance, he wanted Connor to remain in radio communication with Kyle on a secure channel. Consequently, every so often Connor would hear a burst of radio chatter in his ear as each Secret Service post reported in.

"Bravo Three to Bravo One. All clear."

"Ten-four," acknowledged Kyle. *"Bravo Four, send update—"*

"I thought it would be a real drag looking after yet another summer exchange guest," admitted Alicia as Connor suddenly became aware that she was talking to him. "But you're like no other boy I've met..."

She was dancing closer, her deep brown eyes gazing into his. With the dance in its final hour, the band had slowed the pace, and several couples were already slow dancing. As Alicia swayed closer to him, Connor sensed her intentions might be heading in the wrong direction. *Or is it the right one?*

He certainly enjoyed her company, and to say Alicia was pretty was an understatement. But such feelings were close to the line no bodyguard should cross. Indeed, Colonel Black had threatened dismissal of any guardian who entered into a relationship with their Principal. It was a matter both of security and of client confidence.

The president's daughter was now dancing toe-to-toe

with him. Connor could smell her perfume, and with each passing moment, he found his resolve weakening. He could be mistaken, but there was every indication that Alicia wanted to become more than just friends. Whether that was because of his valiant defense of her the previous weekend, because she genuinely liked him, or simply because he was the first boy her father apparently trusted around her, the situation presented a problem. Connor had been concerned that Alicia would find out he was a bodyguard, whereas the real danger was her falling for him. *And me for her . . .*

The song came to an end. They stood awkwardly opposite each other, both unsure what the next move should be.

Connor broke the tension first. As the band counted in another slow number, he asked, "Would you like a . . . drink?"

"Sure," she replied, her hesitant smile unable to disguise what she'd really hoped he'd ask. "I'll . . . um . . . go see how Kalila's getting on with her 'date.'"

Connor watched Alicia walk away. As she reached the edge of the dance floor, she glanced back over her shoulder at him, a fond look in her eyes. He offered what he trusted was a reassuring smile, then headed to the punch-bowl table. He was halfway there when he noticed Ethan and Jimbo having an intense discussion at a nearby table. Their two dates sat with them, ignored and appearing as though they wished they'd never come.

Deciding it was best to avoid another confrontation,

Connor diverted his course and stepped out through the gym's main doors. He judged that it would be okay to leave Alicia for a short while. She was among her friends, and Secret Service agents were patrolling the grounds outside the building.

Passing the bathrooms, Connor turned left to pace a dimly lit corridor and ponder his dilemma over Alicia. *Who could blame me for liking her?* She was fun, gorgeous and the daughter of the *president of the United States*! Such a combination would be hard for any teenager to resist. Especially when *she* was the one showing interest. Under any other circumstances, he'd have jumped at the chance.

No! Connor told himself. He'd made a promise to President Mendez—on his father's memory—to protect Alicia. And he couldn't do that if he got involved with her. Besides, as soon as anyone found out, he'd be transferred back to England—that is, *if* he survived the wrath of her father first. Then Colonel Black would boot him out of Guardian and all the care provided for his mum and gran would be taken away.

With regret, Connor knew he'd have to harden his heart and maintain a respectful distance. The easiest solution would be to say he had a girlfriend back in England . . . Charley, for instance. That would also help explain the international calls he kept making. As he resigned himself to his decision, Connor became aware of a figure at the far end of the corridor. Presuming it was one of Kyle's agents, Connor raised a hand and said, "How's it going?"

Without a word, the figure turned away and disappeared around the corner.

His suspicions aroused, Connor hurried after him. But the adjoining corridor was empty. Connor walked back to where the figure had been standing. There was a row of lockers. One of them was numbered 235—Alicia's locker. It didn't appear to have been tampered with, but Connor was taking no chances.

He pressed a finger to his covert earpiece.

"Bandit to Bravo One," he whispered, using his designated call sign.

Kyle's voice immediately responded. *"Bandit. Go ahead."*

"I spotted a suspect in the east corridor but lost him. He was looking at Ali—" Connor corrected himself. "Nomad's locker."

"I'll send an agent to investigate. Stay with Nomad. Bravo One out."

"There you are!" cried a voice.

Connor spun to see Darryl walking toward him.

"Who were you talking to?" he asked, looking around the deserted corridor.

"Uh . . . just myself," Connor replied.

Darryl gave him a dubious look. "They're about to an-nounce the prince and princess of the school dance, and

Alicia's asking where you are. You haven't seen Fariq, have you? Kalila said he went to make a phone call and isn't back yet."

Connor shook his head.

"What a weird guy he is!" remarked Darryl as they made their way into the gym and over to Alicia and the others. The students were all gathered in a mass before the stage. The band had stopped playing, and the principal was addressing the school.

"By popular vote, this year's prince and princess are . . ."

"You got here just in time," Alicia whispered to Connor, not seeming to notice that he'd forgotten the drinks.

The principal fumbled with an envelope. The students grew quiet in anticipation, and the drummer began a crescendo drumroll.

". . . Connor Reeves and Alicia Mendez!"

The room erupted with applause, and Alicia hugged Connor in delight. "My knight has become my prince!" she said, laughing.

Connor was taken aback by the tribute. He hadn't even known what a school dance prince or princess was until this evening.

Grace winked at Connor. "Nothing like a bit of superhero action to win the vote."

Paige threw some confetti over them and whooped, "Congratulations!"

"You deserve it," said Kalila, her face lighting up for the first time that night.

"Now if you'd like to come up on stage," said the principal, beckoning to the honorary couple.

The crowd parted, creating a corridor on the dance floor for Connor and Alicia. The band launched into the classic "Celebration" by Kool & the Gang, and the two of them danced their way toward the stage. On either side, students clapped and hollered. Alicia beamed with joy, clasping Connor's hand tightly. Connor was also caught up in the infectious atmosphere as party poppers went off and a loud bang triggered a cascade of silver glitter, streamers and balloons from the ceiling.

His earpiece crackled into life. *"Bravo Four to Bravo One. No intruder in east corridor. Just a couple of kids in the locker room. Continuing search . . ."*

Then, out of the corner of his eye, Connor glimpsed the muzzle of a gun.

9

For a split second, Connor's mind froze. Time seemed to grind to a halt. Amid the cheering crowd, falling glitter and tumbling balloons, the ominous black barrel of a handgun poked out between two oblivious students. Aimed at the school dance princess, the deadly weapon seemed to grow in size as Connor focused all his attention on it. The roar of student applause faded like a rapidly receding wave until he heard only his heart beating . . . *THUMPthumpTHUMP-thumpTHUMPthump* . . .

The moment of truth had come.

Deep within him, he heard Jody's voice bawl, *"A-C-E!"*

Assess. Counter. Escape . . .

Suddenly time speeded back up as his bodyguard training kicked into gear. Within a matter of milliseconds he'd assessed the threat and decided on his course of action.

"GUN!" shouted Connor, grabbing Alicia and shielding her with his body.

At first, the crowd looked bemused, uncertain they'd heard right.

Then a girl spotted the barrel too and started screaming. Like the spread of wildfire, the crowd panicked and fled in all directions. There was a *BANG* and Connor tensed, expecting a bullet to hit him. When none did, he crouched low, holding Alicia to him, and ran as fast as he could.

"This way!" he yelled, heading for the nearest exit.

Alicia, utterly bewildered by the sudden turn of events, had no option but to obey.

Two more *bangs* went off. Total chaos ensued. Tables were knocked over. Drinks spilled. Glasses shattered. People collided and began falling over themselves. Connor kept a firm grip on Alicia as he cleared a path through the hysterical students. But his first choice of exit had become blocked as too many people tried to escape through the narrow doorway.

Connor directed Alicia behind an overturned table to reassess his options.

"Where's the gunman?" she asked, her voice trembling with fear.

"Stay down," Connor instructed, trying not to make her a target. It was impossible to see where the shooter was hiding among the frantic crowd. Their closest exit was now at the rear of the stage. But that meant going up the steps and exposing themselves to the gunman.

At that moment, Secret Service agents burst into the gymnasium. Weapons armed and at the ready, their forbidding appearance created even more panic and sent the students scattering. But the highly trained agents kept level heads as they scanned the gym for the threat.

"DROP IT!" shouted an agent on the far side, aiming his SIG Sauer P229 at a figure in the crowd.

Surrounded on all sides by the Secret Service, the gunman threw his weapon to the floor.

"Don't shoot me!" cried a stunned and terrified Ethan, holding his hands high above his head. "It's a water pistol . . . just a water pistol!"

10

The hall's main lights came up, and the school principal, who'd dived offstage at the first "shot," attempted to restore calm over the microphone. Secret Service agents had Ethan pinned to the floor. The rest of the students hung around in shocked silence or spoke in hushed tones as they watched their classmate being frisked for further weapons.

"It was meant to be a joke," blubbered Ethan as his hands were cuffed behind his back. "Tell them, Jimbo, tell them."

Connor cautiously rose from behind the table to confirm that the danger was truly over. The Secret Service had the gymnasium locked down, and no one else appeared to be a threat.

"Can I get up now?" asked Alicia, still crouched in his shadow.

"Yes, it's safe," said Connor, helping her to her feet.

Kyle spotted them and came running over.

"Are you hurt, Alicia?" he asked, noticing an ominous dark patch on her ball gown just below her chest.

Alicia shook her head. Then she looked down at herself and groaned, "Aww, but my dress . . . It's ruined."

She inspected the stain on her bodice and a tear where someone had stood on the hem during their attempt to flee.

"That can be replaced—unlike you," said Connor.

Alicia sighed. "It's actually tailor-made. But you're right, I suppose it could have been a *lot* worse."

An agent approached Kyle. "Looks a bit like a Glock 17, but it's a kid's water pistol all right," he confirmed, handing Kyle the evidence. "That idiot filled it with ink for a prank. Said something about wanting to pay the English boy back . . . for stealing his date."

Kyle raised an inquiring eyebrow in Connor's direction and saw a matching ink stain on his jacket. Connor gave a strained smile.

"So what about the gunshots?" Alicia asked, her cheeks flushing now that the agent knew Connor had actually been her date.

"His accomplice burst some balloons," the agent replied, pointing to the remains of one on the floor.

Letting the matter of their supposed date pass, Kyle showed Connor the "gun." In the full glare of the gym lights, it was obvious that the weapon was a plastic toy.

"Sorry. I *thought* it was real," said Connor, feeling like an utter idiot. At the same time, he was glad it hadn't been. Judging by the stain on Alicia's dress, he'd have reacted too late to save her from a real bullet.

"Easy mistake to make in the heat of the moment," replied Kyle. "Many of our agents have been fooled at one time or another. You did the right thing by calling it in."

"I'm *so* angry with Ethan—" Alicia began, glaring in his direction. Then she frowned. "What did you just say? Connor *called it in?*"

"Um . . . It's just an expression we agents use," Kyle replied, quickly trying to backtrack.

Alicia glanced between the two of them, sensing there was something more to it than that. Then she noticed a tiny piece of skin-toned plastic protruding from Connor's left ear. Her eyes widened in recognition. "Is that what I think it is?"

Connor discovered that his covert earpiece had become dislodged during their escape. He pushed it back in and offered a sheepish grin.

"What are you? My *bodyguard?*" said Alicia, half joking.

Connor said nothing. But she saw the truth in his eyes, and her jaw dropped in disbelief.

"You *are!*" she exclaimed. "The son of a soldier . . . martial arts expert . . . your reactions to the gun . . . All this is starting to make sense . . ."

"I can explain," said Connor. "It's not what you think—"

Alicia held up her hand to stop him. "I don't want to hear it. If this is true, then everything you've said to me is a *lie*." Tears of fury welled in her eyes as her anger at Ethan became redirected toward Connor. "You've deceived me. Betrayed our friendship. Can't I trust *anyone* in my life?"

Her lower lip quivered and she began to cry. Connor reached out to her, wanting to explain that out of anyone, *he* could be trusted. With her life.

"*Don't* touch me!" she said, pushing him away. She turned to Kyle. "Take me home, right now."

And, with not so much as a glance back in Connor's direction, Alicia stormed out of the gym.

11

"A *guardian*? Don't make me laugh!" said Alicia, curled up on the sofa in the Oval Office, surrounded by discarded tissues. "The Secret Service has gone *too* far this time."

"It was actually my idea," admitted President Mendez, sitting beside his daughter, trying to comfort her.

"*WHAT?*" exclaimed Alicia, her hands balling into fists as she glared at her father. "*You* hired Connor?"

"Please, honey, there's no need to shout." He glanced toward his secretary's door, hoping she couldn't hear.

"No need! I thought you of all people would understand. That's what you've been saying, anyway. Now I find out *you're* the one behind it."

"A guardian is for your personal safety," President Mendez explained, recognizing his wife's fiery nature in their daughter. "In light of your recent escapades, the nightmare scenario is you getting kidnapped or shot at by some terrorist, criminal or crazed individual. So it was either that or upping the Secret Service protection. And I knew you wouldn't want that."

"I didn't ask for any of this," Alicia said, waving her hand dismissively around the Oval Office. "This is *your* dream."

"And you are an important part of that dream—my *inspiration* to make this a better world," insisted the president, taking her hand in his. "We've always said family comes first. And that's true. But we're the first family too. And with that comes the necessity for the Secret Service. I admit, it's a real pain at times. But no price is too high to protect my family—especially you, my only child."

Alicia pulled her hand away. "So you send someone to spy on me instead!"

President Mendez sighed. "Connor isn't spying. He's protecting you. As he's proved tonight and last week when you ran into those lowlifes."

Alicia bit her lip as she sought a suitable reply.

"Don't you realize he's risked his life for you—*twice*?"

"Yes," admitted Alicia, unable to meet her father's eye. "But that's not the point. I'm entitled to live a *normal* life."

President Mendez nodded sincerely. "And I want you to have your freedom and your youth. I want you to have everyday experiences with friends your own age. But because you're *my* daughter, that is a privilege, not a given."

Alicia turned to him. "You may rule this country, but what right do you have to rule my life?"

"It's true I am the president of the United States, but first and foremost I'm your father."

Alicia let out an incredulous laugh. "Sometimes I wonder if you really understand the toll living in the White House takes on me. As soon as you took office, you were no longer the father I knew and loved. I mean, I have to make an *appointment* to see you! And with Mother always away on her diplomatic business, I'm a virtual orphan. My friends are all I have. And now you're even controlling them."

"I'm glad you consider Connor a friend—"

"Connor, a *friend*? My night has been ruined because of him. I've been humiliated in front of my true friends. And now, thanks to you, I don't know which of them I can trust."

"You can trust Connor," replied President Mendez. "I certainly do. His father saved my life."

"This isn't about you!" snapped Alicia. "It's about *me*. My life." She rose to her feet in anger. "And I *never* want to see that boy again."

12

Connor stood outside the Oval Office. He could hear the fight through the door. It was too muffled to make out precisely what they were saying, but the gist of the argument was clear. He felt dreadful for having deceived Alicia. She lived under the watchful eye of the Secret Service day and night, and she cherished the rare moments away from its scrutiny. Now she'd discovered he was one of them too and there'd been no real privacy after all.

Yet whether she liked it or not, Connor recognized that Alicia *needed* close protection. Aside from the incident with the two gangsters, Ethan's prank demonstrated just how easy it would be for a gunman to shoot her. In the light of that possibility alone, it was clear that Connor's role as a covert bodyguard was more than justified.

But did the *right* reason warrant the *wrong* lie?

The door to the Oval Office swung open and Alicia came out, fuming. She saw Connor and tried to avoid him.

But Connor made a move toward her. "I wanted to tell you the truth, but—"

"I've had enough of you, Connor," she cut in, her stare cold and hard. "I don't want you talking to me or even near me. You were *hired* to be my 'friend'—my buddy! And you know the worst thing? I"—a tear ran down her cheek—"I was actually falling for you."

The words hit Connor harder than a punch. He realized he'd done more than deceive Alicia—he'd broken her heart. *Sorry* wouldn't be nearly enough to make up for that. But, lost for any other words, he could only watch her as she walked away, sobbing.

"Made quite an impression, didn't you?"

Connor spun around to find Dirk Moran standing behind him. He wasn't sure whether the director had heard Alicia's confession or not. But judging by the triumphant smirk on his face, Dirk appeared to be savoring Connor's fall from grace.

"After you," said Dirk, ushering Connor into the Oval Office.

The president was slumped in his chair, pinching the bridge of his nose as if to ease a headache. "Take a seat. George will be with us in a moment."

Connor perched on the sofa opposite Dirk. No one spoke, and Connor felt the tension in the air. It seemed he'd upset not only Alicia, but her father too.

The chief of staff entered and closed the door behind him.

"It's been quite a night by all accounts," he remarked, sitting down beside Connor.

"The situation was inevitable," said Dirk, his tone sympathetic rather than scathing. "Connor's inexperience resulted in an error of judgment, and he's paid the price. The Secret Service will miss his presence, but what more can I say?"

Despite his words and manner, the director didn't look too cut up about the situation.

"Come, come, Dirk, we've all made mistakes," replied George. "Remember when you thought the Russian ambassador was planting a bomb and it turned out to be his cigar case?"

Dirk shifted uncomfortably at the recollection of that embarrassing incident. Recovering his composure, he responded, "But now that Connor's cover has been blown, the only course of action is to return him to the UK."

"Surely that's an overreaction," said President Mendez. "Connor's presence has been invaluable. We can still use his skills, can't we?"

The chief of staff nodded in agreement. Dirk was about to protest further, but Connor interjected. "Mr. President, I think the director's right," Connor admitted, much to Dirk's astonishment. "I'm sorry. I tried my best, but I can't see Alicia wanting me around any more. I'll pack my bags."

"No, Connor, this isn't your fault. I take full responsibility," insisted President Mendez. "Perhaps if I'd been straight with my daughter from the start, we wouldn't be in this mess."

"Don't be so hard on yourself, Mr. President," said George. "It was your daughter's exploits dodging the Secret Service that forced our hand. And we went through all the options. A secret bodyguard was clearly the best solution. And Alicia is better embarrassed than dead. Once she calms down, I'm sure she'll see sense and get used to the idea of a full-time guardian."

Dirk coughed politely. "I don't see the point of a guardian now. I mean, the Secret Service covers all angles of her security. What advantage does Connor have over one of my highly trained agents?"

"Age," George reminded him. "Connor can *still* go where your agents can't. Alicia may know the truth now, but no one else is going to suspect he's a bodyguard."

"But since Alicia won't accept having him around, he can't do his job in the first place," Dirk argued.

"With great reluctance, I'm starting to side with Dirk on this one," said the president. "Alicia's headstrong like her mother. I can't see her changing her mind any day soon."

President Mendez leaned forward on his desk, his hands clasped together, and looked Connor in the eye. "Connor, you've done Alicia and me a great service. And I can say, hand on heart, your father would be proud of you. But I'm truly sorry—I'll have to send you home."

13

Sitting on his bed in the White House guest room, Connor stared glumly out across the Washington skyline. The National Mall was bathed in bright morning sunshine, but the promising summer day did little to improve his mood.

Operation Hidden Shield had come to an abrupt and humiliating end.

Despite the president's kind words, Connor couldn't help feeling that he'd failed. Although Alicia was physically safe and unharmed, he'd hurt her more deeply than any knife or bullet. And it was infuriating that she'd found out about his role by him protecting her from a *water pistol*! That mistake, as Dirk had rightly pointed out, had cost him dearly. Maybe if it had been a real gun, the outcome would have been different. Alicia would have been thankful for his presence rather than resentful. Then again, he reminded himself that he'd reacted too late to the threat, so he'd failed in his duty anyway. And even if she had survived the attack, she would have always thought their friendship had been based on a lie. That he was "employed" to like her—which in his heart couldn't be further from the truth.

Connor clasped his father's key fob in one hand. Looking down, he studied his father's face. "I'm sorry, Dad. I hope I'm not a disappointment to you," he whispered. "Maybe I'm just not cut out to be a bodyguard."

He clipped the key fob to his backpack of Guardian gear, then began throwing the rest of his belongings into his suitcase. He was almost finished when his phone rang and the Guardian logo flashed on the screen.

Connor had been dreading this call—having to explain to Colonel Black why the assignment was over. He knew the colonel had pinned high hopes on him. A successful operation for the United States government would have boosted the reputation of his organization dramatically.

Taking a deep breath, he pressed Accept, and Colonel Black's craggy face appeared. Connor braced himself for an earful.

"We've received the Secret Service's report," he growled. "What's your side of the story?"

Connor related the events of the previous evening.

Colonel Black nodded and rubbed his chin thoughtfully. "The director's comments do seem overly harsh. And we knew we'd hit this problem sooner or later. It just came a little sooner than any of us expected. Have you tried convincing the president's daughter of the value of a guardian? She has more freedom with you than she would ever get under adult agent supervision."

"There hasn't been the opportunity," replied Connor. "And it's a little more complicated than that."

"What do you mean?"

"Alicia . . ." He searched for the right words. ". . . took a liking to me."

Colonel Black shook his head in despair. "Puppy love!" he sighed. "It'll be the downfall of this organization."

"But I didn't encourage her or—"

"Listen, Connor, I don't blame you for what's happened. And neither should you blame yourself. Being a bodyguard is one of the toughest jobs in the world. And being a *guardian* is even harder. So let's put this assignment behind us and move on. You're to return to HQ for further training."

"Yes, sir," replied Connor, relieved he hadn't been entirely chewed up and spat out by the colonel.

"I'm going to hand you over to Charley now. She's made all your travel arrangements."

Charley appeared, her expression serious and her tone businesslike. "I've e-mailed your itinerary and e-ticket. Your flight is at 1600 hours out of Dulles International. A car will pick you up at 1200 hours."

She glanced off-screen and Connor heard a door close.

He guessed Colonel Black had left the room. When Charley looked back, her sky-blue eyes had softened.

"Don't beat yourself up over this, Connor," she said, keeping her voice low. "The first assignment is often an ordeal. And I don't need to tell you my last one was a complete nightmare. But we *do* get decent assignments. Jason's currently in the Caribbean working protection on a client's beach vacation. His updates consist mostly of the progress of his suntan."

Connor managed a weak laugh. "Lucky for some, I guess. But I doubt the colonel is going to send me on another mission anytime soon. And I'm not sure I could face one after upsetting my Principal so badly."

Hearing the heartache in Connor's voice, Charley replied, "Look, your flight isn't until this afternoon. Why don't you find Alicia and speak to her?"

"She doesn't want to talk ... or even be anywhere near me."

"That was yesterday. Maybe she's cooled off by now. You need to make amends. Otherwise you'll never forgive yourself. Explain to her what it means to be a guardian and why you did it. You never know, she might change her mind. And if not, she'll at least know your intentions were good."

Connor nodded, knowing Charley was right. He needed to say good-bye properly. He wanted Alicia to know how much her friendship meant to him and that it had been real—not just a part of his job description.

14

Ending the connection to Charley and leaving his bags on the bed, Connor went to look for the president's daughter. But she wasn't in her bedroom. Nor was she in the solarium on the third floor. Nor her favorite getaway—the rooftop terrace. He checked the gym, music room, other guest bedrooms and even the linen closet. But to no avail.

Spotting a passing Secret Service agent, Connor asked the man if he'd seen her.

The agent shook his head. "Sorry, not part of my detail today."

"Do you happen to know if she's gone out?"

"No idea," replied the agent. "But I can check for you."

The agent radioed in his request. A minute later, he received a response. "No, not according to her schedule," he said.

"Thanks," said Connor, racking his brains to think where she might be.

He headed to the ground floor, reasoning the Library would be as good a place as any to escape unwanted company. He passed a tour group on the stairs making their way up from the State Floor. A few glanced curiously in his direction, but most were gazing in awe at the Grand Staircase with its glass-cut chandelier and portraits of twentieth century presidents from Truman to Nixon.

Alicia wasn't in the Library. But that was no surprise to Connor now that he'd discovered that the White House was open to tour groups that day. Thinking of all the other places she might be, he tried the movie theater, the dining room, then the bowling alley. He looked everywhere he was permitted to go. Because the general staff weren't aware of his dismissal yet, none questioned his movement through the White House.

Growing more concerned about Alicia's whereabouts, Connor went outside to search the grounds. Aside from the expected roaming patrols, the tennis and basketball courts were deserted. So too were the putting green and children's garden. He asked one of the sentry agents if he'd seen Alicia.

"Negative," he replied.

On Connor's urging, he radioed the other patrols.

"None of the gates report that she's left the premises. Have you checked the swimming pool? Otherwise, she's probably inside the main residence."

"Of course, the swimming pool!" said Connor, hurrying off.

But Alicia wasn't there either.

Connor finally decided to call her. He hadn't tried before, since he doubted she'd answer when his number came up. His assumption had been right. His call went straight to voice mail: *"Hi, you've reached me! If you're calling this number, you know who I am. So leave a message after the beep . . ."*

"Hi, it's Connor, I want to apologize for . . ." He hated answering machines and couldn't think of what to say that wouldn't sound crass or pathetic. "Look, just ring me back." He ended the call.

At this point he was on the verge of giving up. Then Connor remembered the tracking device that was planted in Alicia's phone cover. *For emergency use only,* Amir had said. Connor judged that "Principal missing" qualified as an emergency. Unlocking his smartphone, he pressed the green target icon. The phone froze and he had to reboot. But on the second attempt the Tracker app popped up on the screen.

The map zeroed in on Washington, DC, and his green locator flashed steadily beside the swimming pool. Almost immediately a reassuring red dot appeared within the White House. He zoomed in closer.

Alicia was in the Lincoln Bedroom.

He must have just missed her in his earlier search. The Tracker app outlined the quickest route. Connor hurried back inside and upstairs to the second floor.

Entering the plushly furnished room, he called out, "Alicia?"

There was no answer.

"Alicia! Are you there?" said Connor as he wandered around the room. He checked the adjoining bathroom, opened the walk-in closet, and even looked under the bed. But she was nowhere to be found.

Connor rechecked the Tracker app. It had frozen again. He tapped the screen, but the phone was obviously malfunctioning.

"So much for Amir's 'showpiece,'" he muttered, rebooting and dialing his friend's number.

After four long-distance rings, Amir answered. "Connor! Are you all right? I heard the assignment's nosedived."

"Yeah," replied Connor. "It's not good. But I can't find Alicia to apologize, and your super-smartphone keeps glitching. The Tracker app won't work."

"Really?" said Amir, surprised. "It's probably an I-D-eight user problem."

"What?"

"I'll translate—an i-d-iot user problem."

"Ha-ha," said Connor, "but I'm not in the mood for jokes."

"Sorry, bud, I'll get Bugsy to take a look," he replied. "We can remote access it from here. It may take a while to fix, though. I'll give you a call when it's finished. Just don't switch off your phone."

"Thanks," said Connor. "I'd really like to say good-bye to her before I leave."

Connor slipped the phone into his pocket and wandered over to the window. He looked out across the South Lawn toward the soaring needle of the Washington Monument.

Where are you, Alicia?

As he turned away, his foot knocked something. Glancing down, he saw the red Armani case with its butterfly logo on the floor. It had been snapped in two and now lay in pieces, partly concealed beneath the drapes. Connor guessed Alicia must have thrown it across the room in a fit of anger.

But then another possibility occurred to him, and he felt a knot of dread tighten in his gut. Without wasting another second, Connor headed straight to the West Wing and down to the in-house Secret Service office.

Dirk Moran was there briefing an agent.

Connor knocked on the open door. "I can't find Alicia."

"The president's daughter is no longer your concern," Dirk replied, dismissing him irritably with a wave of the hand. He returned to briefing his agent.

Connor stepped inside. "No, I mean, I've looked throughout the White House and she's *nowhere.*"

The director snorted. "That's probably because she doesn't want to see you. And neither do I."

"But what if she's run away again? Or worse—been kidnapped?" pressed Connor, unable to believe the director wasn't taking his claim seriously.

Dirk glared at him. "The White House is one of the most secure buildings in the world. No one gets in or out without the Secret Service knowing. *We* are professionals. Now go and play *guardian* elsewhere and stop wasting my time."

With that, he pushed Connor out and slammed the door in his face.

15

Connor stood outside the North Portico of the White House, his suitcase beside him and his backpack slung over one shoulder. His departure was definitely less grand than his arrival. Aside from the obligatory Secret Service agent posted at the door, he waited alone for the car to turn up and take him to the airport. No one had come to say good-bye, the president and chief of staff having done so at the meeting the night before and the director of the Secret Service wanting nothing more to do with him. He hadn't expected to see Kyle, because he was off-duty today with the rest of his shift team. But he had hoped that Alicia might appear.

Connor couldn't stop worrying about her. Whatever Dirk Moran believed, he was convinced that she was no longer in the White House. And, as though a storm were brewing on the horizon, he sensed that something wasn't quite right.

The president's daughter is no longer your concern.

Despite the truth of the director's words, Connor still felt responsible for her. And he really didn't want to leave without confirming she was safe.

But he'd run out of time. In a little less than four hours he'd be on a flight back to England.

His phone rang. He snatched it from his pocket, hoping that it would be Alicia.

"We sourced the problem," said Amir on the other end of the line. "Your phone was infected with a virus."

"But I thought you said it had an impenetrable firewall."

"Yeah, but this virus is cutting-edge," Amir replied, his tone implying admiration as well as concern. "A 'Cell-Finity' bug drilled through our firewall code. Fortunately, Bugsy had installed a secondary spyware program that blocked it from spreading. The glitching you experienced was the attempt by the virus to break through."

"What was it trying to do?" asked Connor.

"Bugsy says it allows a hacker—using a secret access code—to connect to the infected phone without the user knowing. The hacker can then monitor all calls, intercept and block texts, and even switch on the microphone to eavesdrop on private conversations. The phone essentially becomes a silent spy."

The storm Connor had sensed on the horizon suddenly felt a whole lot closer. "Who would have planted it? The Secret Service?"

"Possibly, but the unusual coding suggests a *foreign* source.

And that's not the worst of it," continued Amir. "This particular bug sends out a tracer signal. As long as the phone is on, the hacker can track the movements of the user."

"So you're saying someone's been following me, reading my texts and listening to everything I've said?"

"No," replied Amir. "The virus didn't take hold."

"So my phone's okay now?"

"Yeah, we've reinstalled the entire OS from scratch, but a virus like this is easily transferred via the Internet, through an app or even by a simple text message. Our guess is you weren't the intended target and your phone contracted the bug from the person who is."

"*Alicia!*" gasped Connor. "I still haven't been able to find her."

"Well, you can now that the Tracker app is working," Amir reminded him.

"No, I can't. I found the phone case smashed to bits. So, although I can't find her, someone else can."

"That's not good."

Connor waited while Amir related the bad news to Bugsy.

"We might have a solution," said Amir, coming back on the line. "Bugsy's going to try to hack into the Cell-Finity program. If he can reconfigure the coding, break the access code and 'mirror' the signal, then theoretically we can track the target phone too."

"How long will that take?" asked Connor.

"He reckons at least an hour."

"I've a feeling that might be too late."

"Look, I'll call you as soon as we make any progress. And remember: we don't know for certain if Alicia's the one being tracked."

"That's not a gamble I'm willing to take," replied Connor, and he hung up.

Knowing that Dirk Moran would refuse to see him, Connor was on his own until Amir could get proof. In that time, anything could happen to Alicia. He had to warn her.

Opening his contacts, he dialed Alicia's number. But his call went straight to voice mail again. He left another message—more urgent this time.

As he considered what his next move should be, a tour group spilled out of the North Portico's doors. Watching them go past and head toward the northeast gate, it dawned on Connor how Alicia might have left the White House undetected.

16

Alicia stuffed her platinum-blond wig back into her bag. The sweltering summer's day made it too hot to wear. But she kept her Jackie Onassis–style sunglasses on. They were large enough to conceal her features so she wouldn't be immediately recognized.

After leaving the tour group in Lafayette Square, she had darted through a warren of back streets to get more distance between herself and the White House. Now clear of its oppressive shadow, Alicia finally felt able to breathe. She was free of all the surveillance cameras, patrols and restrictions that made her life a virtual prison sentence. She was free of the Secret Service. Free of her father's control. And free of . . . Connor.

After discovering he was her bodyguard, she simply couldn't take it anymore. She felt the walls closing in and desperately needed her own space.

Her phone rang. Alicia looked at the screen and saw Connor's name.

"Why can't you just leave me alone?" she muttered, stabbing the screen with a thumb and rejecting the call.

A moment later her phone buzzed, indicating a voice mail. Alicia ignored it. She didn't want to hear his voice. It would just make her cry again. She couldn't comprehend how Connor could betray her like that. Pretending to be her friend, while all the time working for the Secret Service. She wouldn't be so upset if she didn't like him so much. But he'd worked his way into her heart, and even *now* she was missing his reassuring presence.

No! she told herself. *He lied to me from the start*

"Watch where you're going!" snapped a suited businessman as Alicia almost collided with him.

Looking up from her phone, Alicia discovered she was at the banks of the Potomac River. She'd had no real destination in mind when leaving the White House beyond simply escaping. But as she wandered along the towpath, Alicia realized that, more than her freedom, she desperately needed a friend to talk to. One she could trust.

Alicia thumbed a text into her phone.

Really need to see you. By river near Nat Mall. Can you meet me asap? A

Her phone beeped a few seconds later.

Of course. Jefferson Memorial? 15 mins. K

Alicia smiled with relief. She could always rely on Kalila.

17

The phone in Bahir's hand buzzed. He read the message.

I'll be waiting on the steps. A

Bahir turned to face Malik in the passenger seat of their blacked-out vehicle. "Eagle Chick has taken the bait."

"All according to plan, then," said Malik. "And you're certain her messages have been blocked?"

Bahir nodded with a self-satisfied grin. "Absolutely. My Cell-Finity bug gives us *complete* control of her phone. We can falsify all text messages. Govern every in- and outbound call. Even if she tries calling Kalila now, the line will ring as if engaged."

"Good work, Bahir," said Malik. "You certainly excelled in the task I set."

He looked over at Hazim in the driver's seat. "And well done, Hazim, for planting the bug in the first place."

Hazim managed an anxious smile as Bahir announced, "Target is five minutes out."

Bahir showed Malik the tablet PC in his lap, where a red dot traced its way slowly across a digital map of Washington toward the Jefferson Memorial.

"Then it's time," said Malik, licking his lips in anticipation as he took the prepaid cell phone Bahir offered him.

Hazim started the engine and gripped the steering wheel tightly. He looked out through the tinted window at the memorial with its iconic white marble Greek columns, domed roof and wide stone steps that led down to the water's edge. They had patrolled the location on several occasions, starting with simple drive-bys to identify perimeter protection, security cameras and access control. Then they'd progressed to on-site surveillance. Disguised as tourists, they'd photographed the memorial from every angle, observed the patrol patterns of the park rangers and planned their escape routes. Even the traffic flow around the monument had been monitored. Nothing was to be left to chance.

Hazim pulled out into the traffic and began their slow approach.

"This day the Brotherhood will strike back against the American tyranny over our land and brothers," Malik declared with zealous pride. "This day will mark the turning point in our war on the West."

He flicked open his phone and began dialing . . .

18

Connor stepped through the northeast gate, past the sentry and onto Pennsylvania Avenue. No one questioned him as part of the tour group. Which meant no one would have questioned a *disguised* Alicia either. Connor now realized he'd actually seen her on an earlier tour. She'd been on the Grand Staircase, her back to him, pretending to study a portrait of President Nixon. But he'd been in such a rush and so focused on finding a dark-haired Alicia that his gaze had shot straight past the unassuming girl in jeans with the platinum-blond bob.

Standing at the entrance to Lafayette Square, Connor wondered which direction Alicia might have gone. Without the tracker, it would be like searching for a needle in a haystack. But he guessed she'd try to meet up with one of her friends.

Unlocking his phone, he called Kalila. "Hi, Kalila. It's Connor."

"Hi . . . uh . . . Daisy," answered Kalila, giving a nervous laugh. "That was some dance last night. You and Alicia left pretty quickly afterward. Are you all right?"

"It's a long story," replied Connor. "But I was wondering if Alicia was with you. Or had called?"

"No, sorry. Is anything wrong?"

Not wanting to worry her unnecessarily, Connor said, "Not really . . . Can you just let me know as soon as she contacts you?"

"Sure," replied Kalila.

In the distance Connor heard a deep rumble and wondered what it was. "Look, I've got to go."

Hanging up, Connor tried Grace next. Then Paige. But neither of them had heard from Alicia. He was trying to think of who to call next when his phone rang and the Guardian logo flashed on the screen.

"Bugsy's had a breakthrough!" said Amir, his voice tense and urgent. "Alicia's phone is *definitely* being tracked."

"Have you told the Secret Service?" said Connor.

"That's the problem," replied Amir. "We can't get through."

"What do you mean?"

"All hell's broken loose. Washington, DC's being bombed."

"*What?*" exclaimed Connor, his eyes scanning the park for danger. But everywhere appeared calm and peaceful. Then in the background he heard a second ominous rumble and the wail of police sirens.

"Hi, Connor, it's Charley," said a voice on the line. "Intelligence reports a suspected car bomb has gone off at H Street and Ninth."

"That's near Secret Service headquarters!"

"We know. The explosion was detonated right outside the entrance. Hang on—" There was a ping of an incoming message and a muffled gasp. "There's been a *second* explosion, near the Capitol Building this time."

"I just heard it," said Connor, the tourists milling around him still oblivious.

"Connor, it's Colonel Black," said a gruff voice. "Get off the streets now. That's an order."

"But I believe Alicia's somewhere in the city," he replied, "*without* Secret Service protection."

The colonel grunted. "Then it's up to you to find her. Amir, has Bugsy managed to mirror the signal yet?"

"Yes," Amir replied. "He's patching through the tracer code to Connor's phone as we speak."

Launching the Tracker app, Connor watched the map home in on Alicia's location. It showed her approaching the Jefferson Memorial.

"I've got her," he told them.

"Then it's time to do your job," said Colonel Black. "Just keep your head down. DC's turning into a war zone."

"Yes, Colonel," replied Connor, shouldering his backpack.

"Stay safe!" said Charley quickly. "I'll send you threat up-dates."

Taking the route dictated by the Tracker app, Connor sprinted along Pennsylvania and down Fifteenth Street. The Jefferson Memorial was estimated to be over ten minutes away. Running flat out, Connor hoped he could reach Alicia in half that time. Her life might well depend upon it.

19

Sitting on the top step of the memorial, Alicia gazed across the glassy waters of the Potomac's Tidal Basin. Lush cherry trees framed its banks, and families cruised about in paddleboats, laughing and splashing one another. She watched the carefree way the tourists wandered along the footpath and the easy enjoyment of the children running to and fro. Bathed in glorious sunshine, the scene was almost picture perfect.

A couple of teenagers walked by hand in hand, stealing the occasional kiss. Alicia's eyes followed them, envious of the couple's freedom to do as they pleased.

And they would think I lived the privileged life!

Alicia glanced at her watch for the umpteenth time, impatient for Kalila to arrive. She had so much she needed to confide in her friend. The whole guardian issue, her father's lack of understanding and her feelings for Connor crushed by betrayal. Even thinking about the boy brought tears to her eyes.

Blinking them away, Alicia looked up into the cloud-less blue sky. It was then that she noticed a dark column of smoke rising from central Washington.

Alicia gasped, shocked by what appeared to be a massive fire in the heart of the capital.

Then she spotted a second swirl of smoke to the east. Although the sun shone warm and bright, a cold chill ran down her spine.

Other people began to notice the smoke too, and a murmur of unease spread among the groups of tourists dotted around the memorial. There was a distant rumble like thunder, and moments later a third plume of smoke smeared the sky.

"Oh my, what was that?" exclaimed a woman in a white baseball cap.

"Maybe it's a gas explosion," suggested the man next to her.

An elderly gentleman with a cane and a Vietnam veteran badge squinted into the distance. "Sounded more like a bomb to me."

"Ladies and gentlemen, the memorial's being closed," announced a park ranger, ushering people from the massive temple-like structure. "Please vacate the area immediately."

Bewildered tourists began to file out and down the steps.

"The Jefferson Memorial is *never* closed," muttered the elderly gentleman. "This has to be serious."

He glanced down at Alicia. "If I were you, young lady, I'd go straight home."

Beckoning to his wife, he hurried down the steps as fast as his limp would allow.

Alicia looked north in the direction of her home. The White House suddenly seemed very far away. Alone on the steps, the president's daughter felt dangerously exposed. And truly scared. Alicia now realized how stupid she'd been to run off. Reaching into her bag, she pulled out her panic alarm.

20

President Mendez's feet barely touched the ground as he was rushed from the Oval Office by his Secret Service detail. They charged through the door to the Rose Garden and across the South Lawn to the awaiting helicopter. Marine One's blades thudded loudly, and the grass was whipped into a frenzy by the whirling wind. Bundled up the steps, President Mendez just caught a glimpse of his White House staff fleeing the residence. Karen Wright, her dark blond hair streaming behind her, was close on his heels. A moment later, she joined him in the helicopter's main cabin. The director of National Intelligence was swiftly followed by George Taylor and Dirk Moran. The doors shut behind them, and Marine One lifted off.

"Tell me what's going on! Is this for real?" demanded President Mendez as he brushed himself down and straightened his tie.

"The White House has been compromised," Dirk explained. "We've just received notice of another bomb threat."

"A bomb in the *White House!*" exclaimed the president. "How's that possible?"

"We have no idea at this time. But, given the three car bombings, we must assume this is a viable threat."

"Three?"

"Yes, Mr. President," said Karen Wright, holding on to her seat as Marine One banked left to head toward Andrews Air Force Base, where it would connect with Air Force One, the president's official plane and mobile base in a national emergency. "The FBI headquarters was hit barely a minute ago. This is a *confirmed* terrorist attack on our capital."

"Has any group claimed responsibility?"

"Not yet. It's far too early," she replied. "But the National Security Directive is being implemented, and all key government personnel are being secured."

"I gave the order to evacuate the White House," George informed him, panting heavily from his dash to the helicopter.

The president looked anxiously through the window at the White House disappearing into the distance. "Where's my daughter in all this?"

"Do not concern yourself, sir," replied Dirk, who after five fretful minutes had just gotten word that Nomad's locator beacon had been triggered. "Secret Service agents are en route to escort her to a safe house."

21

"That should keep them occupied for a while," Malik said, ending his call to the receptionist at the White House and flinging the prepaid phone out the car window. He watched it sail over the bridge railing and disappear into the Potomac River.

Bahir checked his tablet PC, where large orange dots now blossomed on the screen. "FBI, Secret Service and US Capitol bombs have all been triggered successfully," he announced to Malik's obvious delight. "Early news reports indicate chaos on the streets."

"Wonderful," said Malik, almost sighing with pleasure. "Then it's time to collect our prize."

A radio crackled into life. *"Gamekeeper to Hide. Over."*

Bahir snatched up the receiver. "Send message."

"Eagle Chick is without sparrows. I repeat, *Eagle Chick is* without *sparrows."*

Bahir looked over his shoulder at Malik in triumph. "Fortune favors us."

Then his tablet sounded an alarm and he cursed out loud.

"What's the problem?" Malik demanded.

Bahir tapped away on the electronic keyboard. "My scanner's picked up a distress signal. From Eagle Chick."

"Then block it!"

Bahir feverishly entered more code but shook his head in frustration. "I can't. It's not coming from her phone."

Malik's expression grew thunderous. "Tell Kedar to move in NOW!"

22

His lungs burning, his heart pounding, Connor dashed around the banks of the Tidal Basin. The Jefferson Memorial was in plain sight. Tourists were spilling out of the domed structure and down the white marble steps. His eyes scanned them for any sign of Alicia. He couldn't spot her. But according to the Tracker, she was still there.

His phone buzzed. He glanced at the secure message from Charley.

White House evacuation. Bomb scare. Do NOT return. Head to Safe House Blue 1.

A blue dot—numbered 686—now pulsed on the digital map several blocks east of the Jefferson Memorial on E Street SW.

Connor was stunned by the rapid sequence of events. Like a house of cards, Washington, DC, seemed to be collapsing around him. He'd heard a third explosion rock the capital only a few blocks away as he'd sprinted across the

National Mall. People were bunched together, gazing in stupefied awe at the billowing columns of smoke. Some were fleeing in panic; others were too shocked to know what to do.

Connor just kept running.

With three key targets hit, he knew the odds of a tourist site being next were dangerously high.

Crossing the Outlet Bridge, Connor had entered the final stretch of path to the memorial when he noticed a 4×4 vehicle with blacked-out windows speeding along East Basin Drive. Weaving in between the traffic, it too was headed directly for the Jefferson Memorial.

Connor put on a last burst of speed, his backpack riding high on his shoulders. He fought against the flow of tourists heading the opposite way. The 4×4 disappeared from his line of sight. But Connor was convinced the driver's objective was the same as his—the president's daughter.

He reached the base of the memorial.

"ALICIA?" he shouted, looking left and right among the countless faces of the passing people.

A head turned in his direction. Connor immediately recognized the dark flowing curls and oversized sunglasses.

"Alicia!" he cried in relief as he bounded up the steps two at a time.

"What are *you* doing here?" she demanded, both baffled and upset by his unexpected appearance.

"My job," he replied, grabbing her hand and pulling her down the steps.

But Alicia resisted, tugging her hand free from his grasp. "Connor, you're *not* my bodyguard."

"But I am your friend and we have to leave now!" he insisted.

"I've already alerted the Secret Service," she explained, taking off her sunglasses and giving him a defiant stare. "I don't need your help."

"They'll be too late." Connor's gaze swept the memorial for approaching threats, his alert level firmly at Code Orange. There were fewer tourists now and only a couple of park rangers. The speeding car he'd seen must have pulled up behind the building.

"What do you mean?" asked Alicia, hearing the tension in his voice.

"Your phone, it's bugged. Someone is intercepting your calls and tracking you *now*. And it's not the Secret Service."

A flicker of shock passed across Alicia's face, and then she snorted in disbelief. "Listen, if this is some trick to prove yourself—"

"Far from it," Connor cut in. He pointed to the skyline. "See for yourself. Washington is under attack. I'm sorry I couldn't tell you I was your guardian before. That wasn't my choice. But my friendship is *real*. You have to trust me."

He offered his hand again.

Alicia looked him in the eyes, trying to judge his sincerity.

Under his gaze, her resistance soon crumbled. "I do, I do," she replied, taking his hand.

"Then let's go," said Connor.

The two of them turned to run, but blocking their path were four men armed with submachine guns.

23

"Alicia Mendez, come with us," said the lead man.

They all wore matching black jackets and mirrored sunglasses. Each carried an FN P90 submachine gun and a holstered SIG Sauer P229. Pinned to their jacket collars were identical red badges with the gold five-pointed star of the Secret Service.

"You got here quickly," remarked Alicia.

"We were in the vicinity," he explained.

"And who *exactly* are you?" asked Connor, not willing to let his guard down.

"Agent John Walker," the man replied, flicking open his credentials. "And *you*?"

Satisfied with the agent's ID, he replied, "Connor Reeves."

The agent arched an eyebrow. "We were informed that you'd left." He glanced at the ominous smoke-filled skyline. "Well, you'd best come with us too."

He signaled to his men, who'd been keeping a close watch on their surroundings. "Let's move out."

The four agents swiftly escorted Alicia and Connor down the steps and around the memorial. They followed a tree-lined path to the parking lot. The blacked-out 4×4 was waiting by the curbside, its engine running. As they approached, Agent Walker keyed his palm mic.

"Delta Four to Control. Nomad recovered. Destination update requested. Over."

The agent listened a moment, then keyed his mic again.

"Received and understood, Control. En route to Blue One. Delta Four out." He turned to Alicia. "We're taking you to a safe house," he explained.

As he opened the rear passenger door to the 4×4, its engine died. The driver looked over at his team leader with a bewildered expression.

"It won't start. All the electrics have shorted out—"

Suddenly the ground erupted with a spray of bullets and the 4×4's bodywork rattled as if caught in a hailstorm. One of the agents screamed as he was cut down by the gunfire.

"GET IN!" yelled Agent Walker, shoving Alicia into the back passenger seat.

Connor dived in after her, pushing her down into the footwell to shield her from the deadly shots.

"Stay there," Agent Walker ordered. He went to slam the

door shut, but another blast of bullets ripped across the 4×4's bodywork. The agent grunted in pain, and blood splattered the interior. He slumped forward onto the seat, jamming open the door.

Connor turned to Alicia and saw blood on her too. "Are you hit?" he asked.

She mutely shook her head, unable to take her eyes off the murdered agent. Connor couldn't allow himself to think about the man's sudden and violent death. This was a Code Red situation. He had to focus all his attention on getting Alicia out of the ambush alive.

The gun battle raged on. The driver jumped from the immobilized 4×4 and joined the last of his team in returning fire. Connor risked a glance through the tinted windshield. The enemy had secured good cover, firing from behind the parking lot's concrete barriers. The two agents, on the other hand, were in the open, the immobilized bulletproof vehicle their only protection.

Connor ducked as the windshield thudded under the impact of more rounds. But the bullet-resistant glass held. Then there was an agonized cry as a third agent was downed.

"Radio for backup!" Connor shouted to the driver.

"Radio's dead," he replied grimly, firing off another shot. "And I'm fast running out of ammo."

"Then we'll have to make a break for it," said Connor, realizing that their chances of survival were dwindling. He didn't know what the enemies' intentions were—kill or kidnap—but he couldn't allow either to happen to Alicia. Peering through the window again, he hunted for a possible escape route. Their only option lay in heading back the way they'd come. But the path was totally exposed for about sixty feet until it reached the tree line. Any escape attempt would be little more than a suicidal dash.

Then Connor remembered his backpack.

"What are you doing?" asked Alicia as he hurriedly removed his pack.

"Making a shield," Connor explained, unzipping the panel to double its length. "It's bulletproof."

"I'll give you covering fire," said the driver, acknowledging Connor's intention.

"What about you?" asked Connor.

"Just get Nomad to safety."

Connor gave him a single grave nod in acknowledgment, conscious of the sacrifice this unknown agent was about to make for them. "We'll head for the trees. Are you ready, Alicia?"

She glanced out the door. "We'll never make it," she said.

"Imagine you're at a track meet racing to the finish line," said Connor.

Alicia managed a strained smile. "Okay, but I'm usually not shot at!"

She took a deep breath and steeled herself for the perilous sprint.

"On your mark," said the driver. "Three ... two ..."

Gripping the handle of his backpack, Connor prayed the liquid body armor would do its job.

"... one ... GO!"

24

The driver blasted the enemy with a storm of bullets from his submachine gun. Clambering over Agent Walker's body, Connor bolted out of the car with Alicia. He kept the backpack shield high to protect them as they ran. With his other arm he held her close by his side so she was always in his cover. Their feet pounded in unison across the gravel path.

"Whatever happens, don't stop!" ordered Connor.

They were halfway when they heard the driver's gun give out. There was a rapid return of fire and a pained cry.

But Connor didn't dare look back.

"STOP OR WE'LL SHOOT!" shouted one of the gunmen.

They had just thirty feet to the tree line—eight . . . five . . . The ground beneath their feet spat dirt as a spray of warning fire cut across their path.

Alicia screamed but Connor urged her onward. They were almost there when a barrage of bullets struck the backpack. The brutal impact knocked Connor off his feet. They stumbled the last few feet before collapsing together behind the trunk of an elm tree.

"Are you all right?" Alicia gasped, realizing he'd taken the full force of the hits.

"Yes . . . ," Connor managed to reply. His shoulder felt bruised, but the liquid body armor had stopped the rounds from doing any lethal damage.

Masked gunmen now emerged from behind the concrete barriers and advanced on their hiding place. One of them fired high into the tree line.

"STAY WHERE YOU ARE!" he ordered.

"What do we do now?" asked Alicia.

Connor realized the gunmen intended to kidnap her; otherwise they wouldn't have bothered with warning shots. But they'd equally shown their willingness to use deadly force to achieve their aims, even if it meant wounding Alicia and killing him. Their situation was desperate, whatever decision he made.

"We keep running," he replied, scrambling to his feet.

With the body armor now slung over his shoulder to protect their backs, Connor shepherded Alicia deeper into the cluster of trees. The gunmen gave chase. Connor weaved in between the trunks, hoping to prevent a clear shot. There was a burst of gunfire. Bullets whizzed past, taking out chunks of bark. Splinters rained down on their heads as the two of them powered on. Then, as they approached the main road of Ohio Drive, the trees thinned out and they lost their cover.

"Over the bridge!" shouted Connor.

They raced across. The gunmen were still among the trees. But it wouldn't be long before they had them in their sights again. Connor realized their only hope was to get to the safe house. From what he recalled, it lay somewhere east of the memorial. Searching for the quickest route, Connor spotted an underpass on the other side of the junction of Fourteenth and Fifteenth Streets.

"Through that tunnel!" he directed Alicia.

The traffic was heavy, but with no time to spare, they dashed across the highway. Cars swerved around them. A truck blasted its horn as they were almost mowed down beneath its wheels. Connor heard gunfire and felt a bullet catch the corner of his backpack, spinning him into the side of a passing car. From behind there was a mighty bang and the earsplitting crunch of metal as several vehicles collided. Horns blared and tires squealed as the traffic ground to a sudden halt.

Connor kept his grip on Alicia and they darted into the underpass.

"Where are we going?" she asked, breathing hard.

"To the safe house," said Connor, trying to reboot his phone on the run. But the screen remained blank. "Is your phone working?"

Alicia pulled it from her pocket. "No!"

Damn, thought Connor. *At least she can't be tracked any longer.*

He tried to recall exactly where the safe house was: *6 . . . 8 . . . 6 . . . E Street SW.*

"How far's E Street Southwest from here?"

"Only about four blocks away," replied Alicia.

"Then let's go."

Behind them they heard the shouts of the gunmen echoing through the tunnel.

Alicia now led the way. They crossed the road, jumping the lane divider, and headed along Maine Avenue. They were about to duck into a side street when a blacked-out 4×4 screeched to a halt in front of them. A blond-haired woman wearing a green Secret Service lapel badge jumped out.

"Quick, get in," urged Agent Brooke from Alicia's PES team.

They dived into the rear passenger compartment. She closed the doors behind them and leaped into the front seat. Flooring the accelerator, she drove off at high speed.

Connor looked through the back window. The gunmen had disappeared from view.

"Are we . . . glad to run . . . into you!" Alicia panted.

"You're a hard one to keep track of," replied Agent Brooke, arching an eyebrow.

Connor turned to her. "I thought you were off-duty today, like Kyle."

Agent Brooke gave him a sharp look. "Everyone's called in during an emergency."

"Not that I'm ungrateful," Connor quickly added.

She turned left onto C Street.

"Aren't we going to the safe house?" Connor asked.

"Yes," replied Agent Brooke.

"But isn't E Street the other way?"

"There's a roadblock because of the bombings. We have to go around."

At the traffic lights, she turned left again onto Fourteenth Street. They headed past the junction to D Street and continued on, joining the main highway that led out of Washington. As the Jefferson Memorial came back into view, Connor began to sense that something was wrong. The detour wasn't logical.

"How long until we get to Blue Two, then?" asked Connor.

"About five minutes," replied Agent Brooke.

Connor had called her bluff. The call sign for the safe house was Blue One. It was now that he noticed the color of Agent Brooke's Secret Service badge. The other agents today had been wearing *red* lapel badges. On his first outing with the Secret Service, Kyle had told him the color-coded badges were an important security measure. Any legitimate agents on a protection detail would be wearing matching badges.

Connor reached for Alicia's hand and squeezed it. *We have to get out of here,* he mouthed to her.

Her brow knitted in confusion. *What?* she mouthed back.

"She's NOT Secret Service!" he whispered.

As the traffic slowed, Connor made a grab for the door handle—but discovered it was locked. He threw his shoulder against the door. "Let us out!"

Agent Brooke spun around in her seat. "You're brighter than I thought," she snarled.

Drawing her gun, she shot Connor point-blank in the chest.

25

"I've lost contact!" cried Amir, searching his computer screen for the green dot that represented Connor. But the bird's-eye view of Washington, DC, was devoid of any tracer signal.

Charley sped over from her central workstation in the Guardian operations room. "It may be just a satellite delay."

"No, I've run diagnostic checks. The uplink is fine."

"What about resetting the connection?"

"Already done that. Nothing."

Charley frowned, a bad feeling starting to creep in. "So where was Connor when you lost the signal?"

"Near the Jefferson Memorial," Amir replied, pointing to the location on the screen. "Judging by his movements, he'd made contact with Alicia and was heading to the parking lot. Shortly after that"—he clicked his fingers in the air—"gone!"

"What about the Cell-Finity bug on her phone?" she asked. "We're mirroring the trace, aren't we?"

Amir offered a pained expression. "That disappeared at the same time as Connor's."

Charley snatched up the desk phone and dialed Connor's number. The line sounded a continuous dead tone. She put the phone down.

"You don't think . . . they've been caught in a bomb blast, do you?" Amir asked fearfully.

Charley's face went pale at the thought. She rapidly typed at the keyboard, requesting an update on the Washington attacks. A few seconds later, a confidential security news feed popped up on the screen. She scanned the page, but there was no report of a fourth explosion . . . not yet, anyway.

"During a state of emergency, the government can block all cellular communications," said Bugsy, coming over from his workstation in the corner of the operations room.

"That's not exactly helpful!" remarked Amir.

"There're two very good reasons. One, to stop the spread of panic among civilians. Two, to prevent a cell-phone signal from triggering an explosive device. Nowadays, the remote-control IED is the terrorists' first choice of bomb. The group behind this attack wouldn't even need to be in the city, let alone the country, at the time of the attack."

"So how can we locate Connor and Alicia and find out if they're safe?" asked Charley.

"Have you tried the GPS-tracker that the Secret Service implanted in his watch?"

Amir shook his head. "We weren't given access to that."

Bugsy plunked himself down at his computer terminal. "Shouldn't be a problem to fix," he replied, popping a stick of gum into his mouth and chewing hard. "The tracker will be transmitting on a separate protected frequency."

His fingers rattled across the keyboard as he quickly gained access to the Secret Service Locator program. Leaning back in his chair to study the data, Bugsy scratched his bald head with bemusement.

"Strange . . . Even that's disappeared," he mumbled, half to himself.

On hearing this, Charley picked up the phone again and dialed a different number. She gave her call sign and typed in her security password. "Can you give me confirmation of Nomad's arrival?"

After listening to the response, she numbly put the phone down.

"They're not at the safe house," she informed them. "We need to update Colonel Black. I fear the worst has happened."

26

A body lay in the middle of the abandoned aircraft hangar, a bullet through the head.

"That will ensure her silence," Malik said, grinning and lowering his gun.

"But that agent was one of us!" exclaimed Hazim, his face aghast at the brutal execution.

Malik's expression became stony. "We must tie up all loose ends, Hazim. A double agent can never be trusted."

"Well, what about all those innocent people killed by our bombs? You never told me about that part of the plan. How can we justify those killings to God—"

"Don't you *dare* question my command, Hazim!" snarled Malik, taking a step closer and looking Hazim in the eye. "They were infidels. But I'm beginning to wonder if I should be questioning *your* commitment to the cause."

"No, not at all," Hazim said, shaking his head vehemently.

"I hope not," said Malik. He strode away, leaving Hazim staring at the body of the ruthlessly slain agent.

Malik approached the 4×4 where his men stood guard. Peering into the rear passenger compartment, he admired his prize. The president's daughter was slumped unconscious on the backseat, a tranquilizer dart piercing her neck.

"When the dust settles, Washington will discover what we've *really* achieved," he said, and laughed coldly.

Bahir swept a surveillance scanner over Alicia's prone body. A red light blinked on as the device passed over her jeans pocket. Bahir pulled out the bugged phone.

"A job well done!" he said, congratulating himself on his programming skill with the Cell-Finity bug. He extracted the SIM card and snapped it in half before crushing the phone under his boot.

The scanner flashed again, this time over her bag. He rifled through the contents and pulled out the panic alarm.

"I trust that's not still active?" said Malik.

Bahir shook his head. "The EMP Kedar fired during the attack at the memorial disabled all electronic equipment in the four-by-four's vicinity." He broke apart the alarm case and disconnected the innards. "This sweep is just to make one hundred percent certain."

Bahir now turned his attention to Connor's body. The scanner immediately found his smartphone. Bahir popped out the SIM card and destroyed it. He was about to smash the phone too when he noticed the screen boot up and the graphic of a lock appear.

"That's strange," he muttered. "How can its circuitry still be functioning?"

Intrigued by the anomaly, he checked to be sure there were no outgoing signals, then pocketed the phone for later analysis. He continued his surveillance sweep. The scanner blinked rapidly as it passed over Connor's wrist.

"Someone certainly didn't want to lose this one," he remarked, removing the fancy watch.

"I wonder why that is," Malik mused, leaning in closer to get a better look at Connor's face.

"He's a special guest of the president on an exchange program," Hazim replied flatly as he rejoined the others. "His name's Connor Reeves. He's English."

"Well, he's not invited to our party," said Kedar, drawing his handgun and aiming at Connor's head.

"Hold your fire!" ordered Malik.

"But I thought we agreed no prisoners, apart from the girl."

Malik pushed Kedar's gun away. "No, don't kill him ..." He tugged the tranquilizer dart from Connor's chest. "Not yet, anyway. Having another child hostage might prove a useful bargaining chip."

27

"The White House is all clear, Mr. President," announced George. "The bomb disposal team has swept the residence three times now, and *that* particular threat appears to have been a hoax."

"A *hoax*? The others certainly weren't," replied President Mendez, seated at the head of the conference table aboard Air Force One. The past few hours had been some of the worst the nation had known since 9/11, and he was in no mood for practical jokes.

"This was most likely a prank call, inspired by but unconnected to the bombings," explained Karen Wright. "We couldn't take that risk, though."

"It was the right decision, Karen. But I need to get back into the Oval Office and make a statement to reassure the nation. What's the situation at the other locations in Washington?"

The director of National Intelligence swiped her finger

across her touch-screen computer. An updated situation report appeared on the screen.

"All targeted areas have been cordoned off. Official reports indicate structural damage to Secret Service and FBI headquarters. The US Capitol Building has escaped unscathed. There were one hundred and fifty-four injuries at the last count, but mercifully few confirmed deaths. We can thank the swift response of our emergency services for that."

Karen scanned down the page to the ERT report. "The Environmental Response Teams have completed initial atmospheric analysis. Apart from the anticipated smoke and fumes, no chemical, biological or nuclear compounds were found in any of the attacks."

President Mendez breathed an audible sigh of relief. "A dirty bomb would have been our worst nightmare. So, can we assume the immediate threat is over?"

"It appears that way," replied Karen. "But as a standard precaution we've closed all public buildings and diverted traffic out of the downtown area, and a block-by-block search for any suspicious vehicles or packages is under way. So far, no further danger has been reported."

"Then we can inform the public that we are in control of the situation."

"Yes, Mr. President."

"Excellent. It's important that we display a show of strength against these terrorists."

"I'm afraid it's not all good news, Mr. President," said Dirk, entering the airborne conference room, his face drawn and haggard after a high-priority call from the Joint Operations Center. "As you know, we received confirmation from Delta Four that your daughter was picked up and being taken to a safe house. But—"

"But what?" demanded President Mendez.

"The team never reached the safe house."

President Mendez blinked, unwilling to believe what he'd just heard. "And you've only learned about this now?" He glanced at the clock on the cabin wall. "It's been over *five hours*. Where is she, then?"

Dirk's solemn expression said it all. "The Secret Service team has just been found dead in the Jefferson Memorial parking lot. There was a gun battle."

"Alicia too?" he asked, his hands beginning to tremble. As president he was more than capable of handling a national crisis, but as a father the thought of losing his daughter was too much to bear.

Dirk shook his head. "There was no sign of her."

"So she's still alive?"

"Yes, in all probability," replied Dirk. "I've also been informed that Connor was with her at the time."

President Mendez frowned. "I thought he'd left."

"So did I. But Guardian uncovered evidence at the last

minute that your daughter's phone was tapped and being tracked."

"Then why haven't you found her yet?" asked President Mendez, anguish gripping his heart like a vice.

"Her panic alarm malfunctioned. We lifted the block on cellular calls, but her phone's dead too," explained Dirk. "With Secret Service headquarters crippled by the bomb blast and the current state of emergency, our teams have been stretched to the limit. If we'd only been allowed to put a tracker on her—"

"Dirk, I don't want excuses. I need results," President Mendez barked, pounding the table. "Land this plane right now. Get me back to Washington. Divert every resource available to *finding my daughter!*"

28

A splitting headache was the first sensation Connor was aware of. Then a deep throbbing ache in his muscles. Followed by an unsettling queasiness in his stomach. As he regained full consciousness, he attempted to swallow, but his mouth was dry as a desert and his throat sore and swollen.

He cracked open his eyes, but the light hurt like fire, and indistinct shapes swirled before his vision. When it eventually settled, Connor discovered he was lying on a hard concrete floor. In front of him was a battered plastic bottle of water and a featureless wall. Fighting the heaviness in his limbs, he tried to sit up but was instantly hit by a wave of nausea. He lay still until the feeling passed.

With an immense effort, he managed to prop himself up against the wall. His head swam, and the sickness returned. Reaching for the water bottle, Connor undid the cap and took a swig. It was warm and slightly bitter, but it revived him enough to regain his senses. He had no idea how long he'd been unconscious. It could have been hours or days. But judging by the hunger cramps in his stomach, he'd missed a meal or two.

Looking around, he discovered he was in a small windowless room, a single bare bulb for light. There was a door to his left, flush to the frame and without a handle. To his right lay Alicia, her body discarded like a rag doll on a thin mattress in the corner.

"Alicia!" he croaked.

She didn't respond. Fighting the nausea and pain in his muscles, he dragged himself over to her. Alicia was so still that he thought she was dead. Then Connor noticed a strand of hair across her mouth quivering as she exhaled a shallow breath.

Connor gently shook her shoulder and she groaned, still deep in a drug-induced sleep.

"Alicia, wake up!" urged Connor.

Her eyes wearily blinked open. "Huh?"

"Drink this," he said, pressing the bottle to her lips.

Alicia managed a sip.

"I think I'm going to be sick," she rasped.

"It's just the effects of the tranquilizer, or whatever drug they've given us," explained Connor.

He gave her time to recover, then helped her into a sitting position.

"What's going on?" she murmured, holding her head in her hands.

"We've been kidnapped," said Connor, keeping his voice low. There was no one else in the room, but he didn't want their conversation overheard by whoever had taken them. "What do you remember?"

Alicia tried to think, disoriented by the strange environment. "Um ... you getting shot ... by Agent Brooke. Then she turned the gun on me and it all went dark." She looked up at Connor, her eyes wide, panic bubbling just beneath the surface. "I thought I was ... *you* were dead."

Connor took her hand, trying to calm her. "No, we were just sedated."

"How long have we been out?"

Connor glanced at his wrist, but found that his watch had been taken. "Your guess is as good as mine."

Alicia looked fearfully around the bare, windowless cell. "Do you know where we are?"

"No idea," replied Connor, forcing himself to his feet. But he feared they were a long way from home.

Swaying slightly, he made the five short steps across the room to the door. He tried to push it open. Then he tried to get his fingers around the edges and pull the other way. But it wouldn't budge. Pressing his ear to the door, Connor listened for any noise that might give away their location.

He heard nothing. Just deafening silence. It was as if they were cut off from the entire world.

29

The atmosphere in the White House Situation Room was tense and frantic as Colonel Black was shown his seat at the conference table. Already gathered around the long mahogany desk were the key members of the National Security Council and the head of every relevant security and intelligence agency, all pooling their resources to solve the case at hand. National Security staff worked feverishly in the background, analyzing incoming data and delivering constant updates.

"Good of you to come," said President Mendez, acknowledging Colonel Black's arrival with a firm handshake.

To the colonel's eyes, the president had aged dramatically, his renowned youthful vigor weighed down by a terrible burden.

"It's my honor and duty," replied Colonel Black. "Don't worry, we will find your daughter."

And Connor, he promised himself. He'd never lost a guardian yet, and he didn't intend to now.

The White House chief of staff appeared and handed the colonel a folder. "This contains a summary of all the information we have at present, including your organization's report."

"Thank you," acknowledged the colonel, immediately scanning the files.

"Is there *any* word yet?" asked the first lady, who sat beside her husband, pulling at a frayed handkerchief. She was exhausted from her transatlantic flight home, and her usual glamorous appearance had all but disappeared under the strain, her makeup streaked with anguished tears.

"I'm afraid not, Mrs. Mendez," replied George. "But I can assure you, we're doing everything in our power."

"Well, it's not enough!" she snapped. "It's been twelve hours. Alicia could be anywhere in the world by now."

"That's why we've brought the CIA in on this," Karen said, offering the first lady a glass of water that she took in one trembling hand. "They've put out a worldwide alert to every agent. If they get a sniff of anything, we'll be the first to hear about it."

"That's reassuring to know," said Mrs. Mendez, sipping at the water and trying to regain her composure.

A blond-haired woman with frameless glasses leaned forward and raised her hand. "What shall we do about the press?" asked Lara Johnson, the White House press secretary.

"Keep a lid on it for as long as you can," replied George.

"But we could use them to promote a search for the president's daughter," she suggested.

Karen shook her head vehemently. "Then we'll have every Tom, Dick and Harry phoning in. And any possible lead will disappear under a pile of misguided calls. No, concentrate on the containment of the bombings until we have more concrete information."

"About the bombings," interrupted General Martin Shaw, walking over and saluting Colonel Black. "I think we must assume a connection."

"Why's that?" asked the president.

"The timing, for one. The last contact with Delta team and Alicia's disappearance were just minutes after they detonated. I believe these attacks were merely a *distraction* for the main event."

"A distraction!" exclaimed George. "The three bombs almost crippled Washington."

"Exactly. Their targets were designed to disrupt communications and impede the workings of the Secret Service. With their attention focused elsewhere, the kidnappers had all the time they needed to escape with the president's daughter."

"I concur with the general," said Colonel Black. "It would certainly explain the planting of the Cell-Finity bug and the coordinated ambush on your Secret Service team. Has any terrorist group claimed responsibility yet?"

"Still nothing," Karen replied. "But we're doing an analysis of the most likely candidates—"

"We've got a lead!" Dirk interrupted, coming off the phone.

The Situation Room went silent as he pressed a remote and a live link flashed up on the central monitor. An auburn-haired man with a rounded pockmarked face appeared.

"Mr. President, my name is Agent Cooper," he said. "I'm in situ at an abandoned aircraft hangar near Stafford Airport. My team has discovered one of our off-duty Secret Service agents, Lauren Brooke, shot dead, execution-style."

The camera panned to show a body sprawled across the concrete floor, a pool of dried blood surrounding it. The first lady gasped at the gruesome sight and averted her eyes.

"How does this connect with Alicia's disappearance?" asked President Mendez, a cold sensation creeping into the pit of his stomach.

"My team found the remains of a cell phone that bear her fingerprints." The camera was angled to display the shattered phone. Then an empty 4×4 came into view, surrounded by three agents analyzing the vehicle for further clues. "They've also just confirmed that hairs on the backseat of Agent Brooke's vehicle match your daughter's."

"But is there any sign of my little girl?" asked the first lady, almost dreading the answer.

"No, ma'am," replied Agent Cooper. "But that can only be seen as good news. It indicates that she's probably still alive.

We also found this at the scene." He directed the camera to a backpack lying in the footwell of the 4×4.

"That belongs to Connor," volunteered Colonel Black, recognizing both the design and Justin Reeves's face in the attached key fob.

"Connor, sir?" questioned the agent.

"He's a boy secretly assigned to protect Alicia," Dirk explained. "Part of the Guardian organization."

Agent Cooper raised an eyebrow at this revelation but made no direct comment. "That explains the backpack's unusual construction, then. The rear panel's liquid body armor, and it shows signs of recent combat usage. But there's no blood, so it appears to have been effective."

"That means Connor's still with her," said Colonel Black, feeling relieved that his charge was most probably alive and, at the same time, more optimistic about the survival prospects of the president's daughter. He just prayed that Connor's basic training would be enough to see him through the crisis.

"Looks that way," replied the agent.

"Then there's hope," said the president, squeezing his wife's hand.

The first lady returned a strained smile.

Dirk sighed inwardly at President Mendez's unwavering belief in the boy. "But, Mr. President, it could also mean our problem's doubled . . . if they've *both* been kidnapped."

30

"This is all my fault," sobbed Alicia, her entire body trembling with shock. "I should have listened to the Secret Service . . . If I had, we wouldn't be in this mess. Now I've put you in danger too, Connor. What have I done? I'm sorry . . . I'm so sorry."

Connor knelt before her. He was as scared as she was, but he couldn't allow his own fears to spiral out of control. He had to remain strong—for both their sakes.

"This *isn't* your fault," he assured her. "The blame lies with our kidnappers. What we need to do is stay calm and focused. Your father, the Secret Service, Guardian, *everyone* will be looking for us."

Alicia stared at Connor, her eyes wide and swimming with tears. "Do you really think so?"

"I know so. We just have to hold out until they come."

"But what if they can't find us?"

Connor was aware that that was a distinct possibility, but

replied, "With all the government's resources, they're bound to sooner or later. We have to have faith."

Alicia fell silent and gazed doubtfully around their tiny cell. Connor could see she was battling to keep her panic in check. But she bravely wiped away her tears and managed to stop shaking.

"So who do you think has taken us?" she eventually asked.

"Agent Brooke must have been working for those gunmen," Connor replied. "And with all the bombings I can only guess that they're terrorists of some sort."

"So they're going to . . . kill us?" said Alicia, her voice fragile and desperate.

Connor gently shook his head. "If they wanted us dead, that would've happened already."

"Then what *do* they want?"

Connor heard a bolt unlock and he spun around. "I think we're about to find out."

His nerves taut as a wire, Connor stood protectively in front of Alicia as the door swung open. A colossal man in black robes stepped inside, his bulk almost filling the tiny cell. The man's face was obscured by an all-enveloping coalblack headscarf that left only his dark eyes blazing through at them.

"*Ta'ala ma'ee!*" he growled in what Connor presumed was Arabic.

When they didn't respond to his command, he grabbed

Connor by the arm and shoved him roughly through the doorway. Connor didn't want to be separated from Alicia and struggled in his grip.

"Let me go!" he protested.

But the ferocious glare from the man warned him not to resist any further.

Their captor treated Alicia more respectfully. He gestured for her to leave the cell and follow Connor.

Numbly getting to her feet, Alicia hurried over to Connor's side. They said nothing as they were marched down a short corridor. Connor kept alert to every detail, just as he'd been trained to do. He noticed that their captor wore sandals, his feet were dark skinned and his robes were Middle Eastern in style. There were no windows in the corridor and the air smelled stale and slightly damp, so he guessed they must be underground. In a small room opposite their cell, he'd glimpsed a computer with an array of electronic gadgetry. If connected to the Internet, he might be able to send a message for help—that is, if he found out exactly where they were and *if* he ever got the chance.

At the end of the corridor a flight of wooden stairs led upward into blackness. The temptation to make a run for it was almost overwhelming. Then a second masked man stepped from a doorway, a submachine gun in his grasp. The brief flicker of hope Connor had felt was extinguished in an instant.

Their captor shoved them into the end room. Alicia recoiled in horror as they were greeted by three more faceless men. Two carried assault rifles, and the third brandished a gleaming curved dagger, its bone handle studded with jewels. As threatening as the guns were, the presence of the knife was even more intimidating.

"Kneel!" ordered the man in accented English, pointing to a spot on the floor with his dagger.

On the wall behind was a large black flag with Arabic writing in white. Positioned opposite was a video camera on a stand. Connor felt an icy spike of fear.

Their captors hadn't killed them yet, simply because they intended to do so *live* on camera.

31

Connor knelt next to Alicia, who once again was trembling like a leaf. He couldn't blame her; his own heart was thudding furiously within his chest. Neither of them could take their eyes off the vicious-looking knife as it was waved in front of their faces. The man with the dagger seemed to relish their fear and purposely take his time.

Suppressing his panic, Connor vowed that he wouldn't go down without a fight. However futile the attempt, he'd at least try to save Alicia. It would be what his father would have done in such a situation.

The man, who appeared to be the leader, placed the tip of his knife under Alicia's chin and forced her to raise her head and look him in the eye.

"No need to cry," he declared. "We've no intention of harming you. You are our guests."

Overcoming her abject terror, Alicia stared defiantly back at the man. "That's funny—we didn't get the invite."

The leader grunted a dry laugh. "Ah! American humor. How amusing!"

He sheathed his knife, then clapped his hands once, the sudden noise startling Alicia. A moment later, a tray was brought in and laid before them. Upon it were two pieces of flatbread, a bowl of hummus, a jug of chilled water, some rice and a thick meat stew. As it was presented to them, an awful thought crossed Connor's mind. *Our final meal.*

"Please eat," invited the leader casually, as if they were dining in a restaurant.

Ravenous from the aftereffects of the sedative, Connor and Alicia were unable to resist the offer. Tentatively picking up a spoon, Connor dipped it into the stew and scooped some into his mouth. Simple as the meal was, with death so close at hand, the food tasted almost divine. Alicia joined him, tearing off a piece of flatbread and nibbling at it nervously. But, overcome with hunger, she soon dug in, and they both momentarily forgot their grim predicament.

As they ate, the leader nodded to one of his men to press Record on the video. The camera's light flashed red, and the leader addressed the lens.

"President Mendez, we, the Brotherhood of the Rising Crescent, hold your daughter hostage," he said with an arrogant pride in his voice. "We also have her friend, the English boy. As you can see, they're both well and being looked after according to their status."

He gestured to them with a sweep of his hand, and Connor looked up, his mouth half full. He now realized the meal was purely a show for the camera.

"I'm certain that, as a father and the president of your country, you wish for their safe return," continued their hooded captor. "Their fate very much lies in *your* hands."

Both Connor and Alicia stopped eating, the thinly veiled threat killing all appetite. They glanced anxiously at each other, each wondering if the broadcast was going out live.

Connor thought about shouting out or signing a message, but he knew little of their location—except that they were possibly somewhere in the Middle East—and he knew even less about their captors that would help the Secret Service or Guardian rescue them. He briefly considered an escape attempt while the terrorists were distracted. But one glance toward the doorway, where the gunman stood guard in the corridor, soon dispelled any such illusions. They'd be shot down before they even planted one foot on the stairwell. He was utterly powerless.

Yet, just as he felt a cloak of despair settle over him, Connor suddenly realized that he did have two pieces of information he could communicate on camera. He just had to stay sharp and proceed with caution.

32

"Our demands are simple," said the hooded leader, his image filling the central flat-screen monitor in the White House Situation Room. "You have until midnight on the third of July to release every one of our brothers imprisoned on terrorism charges and to announce the withdrawal of all American troops from the Middle East. Meet the first demand and the boy will be freed as proof of our word. Meet the second and you'll be reunited with your daughter. Those are our terms. This year, the fourth of July will be *our* Independence Day."

The picture froze on Alicia's face. Her expression was defiant, but her complexion was pale, and her eyes shone with barely restrained tears.

A deathly silence fell over the Situation Room. No one even breathed, too stunned by the inconceivable kidnapping of the president's daughter.

Then the first lady let out a sob and the Situation Room was motivated into frenzied action.

"At least we know they're both alive," said Karen, the director of National Intelligence, trying to offer the first lady some comfort. "The video was time-stamped just fifty-eight minutes ago."

"Has this gone public?" President Mendez asked, his voice strangely fragile.

"Not so far as we're aware," replied Dirk. "The video link was sent directly to your secretary's e-mail account."

"That's odd," remarked the press secretary. "Most terrorists want publicity. I'd have thought they'd plaster this across the entire Internet."

"There's no guarantee they won't," said George, grimacing. He popped an antacid tablet into his mouth to ease his heartburn. "It'll all be part of their sick propaganda war."

"Who *are* the Brotherhood of the Rising Crescent, anyway?" General Shaw demanded.

Karen's Middle East adviser, Omar Ahmed, opened a file on his laptop and linked it with the Situation Room's central monitor.

"They're a fundamentalist group, based in Yemen," he explained, pointing to the information on display. "Unrepresentative of the majority of their faith, their stated goal is 'to fight every nonbeliever until victory or martyrdom and to make every American regret their occupation of their lands.' The leader is believed to be Malik Hussain." A grainy picture of an Arab, too indistinct to make out his features, flashed up on the screen. "Born in Sana'a, the capital city of Yemen, to a wealthy oil family, he was educated in Saudi Arabia before heading to Afghanistan to fight with the Taliban. After that he pops up in Pakistan and Iraq until settling permanently in his homeland."

Omar closed his laptop.

"Is that all you have on them?" said General Shaw.

Omar nodded regretfully. "Like many minority extremist outfits, they were under our radar. The CIA simply didn't think they had the resources to launch a viable attack."

"Well, they did!" snarled Dirk. The Secret Service director's jaw was tense with anger.

"Yes, we underestimated this enemy," admitted Omar. "But to coordinate bombings and a kidnapping on this scale, some *other* organization has to be backing them."

"Like who?" asked the president.

Omar shrugged. "These groups function as independent cells. We may never find that out."

There was a heavy silence around the conference table as they considered the grave implications of what Omar had said.

"Our first priority must be to locate and safely retrieve the hostages," said General Shaw decisively. "Have we sourced the e-mail yet?"

"Our analysts are working on it as we speak," replied Dirk. "And technicians are searching for clues in the transmission itself."

"We're also checking every outbound flight within the last twenty-four hours," added Karen. "Charter, private, commercial and business. That should narrow our search."

The president thumped the table in frustration. "How could these people smuggle my daughter out of the country without *someone* knowing?"

"My poor little girl—she must be terrified," said the first lady, fresh tears running down her cheeks.

President Mendez drew his wife into his arms and she wept on his shoulder. "At least Alicia's not alone in her plight. Connor's been trained to handle hostage situations. Isn't that right, Colonel?"

Colonel Black nodded, although he now seriously wished he'd dedicated more time to it in the Guardian syllabus. But he had faith in Connor's resilience. "Connor will be as crucial to your daughter's survival as your team in finding her," he assured them.

Dirk couldn't help a dismissive snort. "Some bodyguard your boy turned out to be," he muttered, evidently cracking under the pressure.

Catching his comment, Colonel Black spun on him. "Well, if you hadn't dismissed him so readily, he might have been able to do his job properly," he retorted. "And, thanks to Connor's intervention, the last ring of defense hasn't been broken yet."

Dirk shot him an incredulous look. "He's a hostage! An *additional* problem."

"Connor's an asset," corrected the colonel, and asked for the video to be replayed. "He's already informed us that they're being held underground and that there are at least five gunmen."

He paused the video and indicated the screen. "See here, Connor's pointing a finger down beneath his hand. And here he forms his fingers into the shape of a gun, then opens his hand to indicate five."

"Are you sure of this?" asked George, scrutinizing the video playback.

"Yes. The movements are very subtle, but he repeats them twice."

"Still, that's not much help," remarked Dirk.

"It's a start," Colonel Black said. "And such information could be crucial for any rescue attempt."

33

Connor had no idea whether anyone would spot his discreet hand signs or even recognize them as signals. But the act itself afforded him a small sense of control over their situation, which helped fend off his feelings of powerlessness.

After the video recording, their captors escorted them back to their cell and locked the door once more. Alicia, who'd fought so hard to hold back tears, collapsed on the threadbare mattress and sobbed her heart out. Connor sat down beside her, put his arm around her shoulders and let her cry.

During Hostage Survival class, Colonel Black had told them they would need to control their emotions, stay calm and keep a level head.

Easier said than done, thought Connor, glancing at Alicia and then around their tiny prison cell. If he didn't have Alicia to protect and look after, he'd probably be falling apart himself.

At the time, the colonel's advice had seemed somewhat hypothetical. Being kidnapped was a situation that would *never* occur—or so Connor had believed. But now that he and Alicia were being held hostage, he had to deal with it.

He tried to recall the other vital pieces of advice Colonel Black had given them.

Don't offer resistance . . . Say as little as possible if questioned . . . Try to stay fit and healthy . . . Keep your mind active . . . Set goals . . . Plan on a long captivity to stave off disappointment and depression . . . And, most important of all, maintain the will to survive.

Colonel Black had reiterated this last point. Despite all temptation to cave in and succumb to despair, it was essential to believe the situation would come to a positive end eventually. Sustaining hope was the key to survival.

"Don't worry, Alicia, we *will* get home," said Connor.

Alicia sniffed and looked up at him, her eyes red from crying. "How . . . can you be so sure?"

"We're worth more alive than dead to our captors. They'll need to prove we're unharmed to get what they want."

Alicia nodded, seeing the sense in his words. "You're right. It's just that the knife and the filming were all too much for me."

"I understand," said Connor, shuddering at the thought of the leader's vicious blade. "But we need to appear strong to these terrorists. We can't let them think they've beaten us."

Alicia sat up and composed herself, tying back her hair and wiping her eyes dry.

"I won't give them that satisfaction," she said, the steel in her voice returning.

"That's more like the Alicia I know," said Connor, smiling.

She returned his smile but struggled to maintain it. "I just can't help thinking about my parents. They'll be beside themselves with worry."

"True," said Connor, his own thoughts going to his mother and gran. If they'd seen the broadcast, they could be utterly devastated too—and they would have the shock of discovering his double life. "But just keep in mind that your father will be doing everything in his power to negotiate our release."

34

"The United States government does *not* negotiate with terrorists," declared Jennifer Walker, the US secretary of state,
who sat opposite President Mendez at the conference table.
She wore a dark green business suit, her auburn hair was cut
short and her face, icy hard at the best of times, was fixed in
a fiercely determined expression.

"But we're talking about my daughter here!" implored
President Mendez.

Jennifer's gaze softened a little. "I'm wholly aware of that,
Antonio. And I'm deeply sorry for your predicament. But
you know full well our position on such matters."

The president sank back into his chair and nodded with
great reluctance. He realized he was no longer acting like
the commander in chief. In truth, he was a father out of his
mind with worry because his little girl was in some grim
basement with a gun at her head. And he would do *anything*
to bring her home.

"Can't we even offer them money?" suggested the first lady, wringing her hands in desperation.

"We could try via an intermediary, but that's not what they're seeking," said Karen.

"Karen's right," concurred Dirk. "If it was only money the terrorists wanted, they'd have selected an easier, less prominent target."

"Surely every terrorist has a price." The first lady looked hopefully around the table for agreement.

Omar shook his head. "The Brotherhood's motives are purely political. We're dealing here with fanatics, willing to kill or be killed for their cause."

The harsh reality of the lengths the terrorists would go to numbed the first lady into silence.

George stepped in. "Then we have to open a dialogue with this group and stall for time to allow our forces the best chance to trace their hideout. As our initial response, we could ask for the names of the prisoners the terrorists want released and what proof they need."

There was some consensus around the conference table at this.

"Perhaps even release some of them in return for Connor," he continued. "The handover might give us vital information on Alicia's location."

"That's too steep a price to pay," argued General Shaw. "We're talking about men directly responsible for 9/11 and

hundreds of dangerous terrorists that our forces have sacrificed their lives to capture. We simply can't contemplate
freeing them to wreak more devastation on our nation."

"As much as I want Connor back, I agree with the general,"
said Colonel Black. "And, given their meticulous planning,
they'll avoid any links to their hideout in such a handover."

"But when this goes public, the pressure from the media and the American people to get Alicia back will be overwhelming," noted the press secretary. "We might have no
choice *but* to negotiate."

"Absolutely not!" countered Jennifer. "If we bow to one
terrorist organization, we'll open the floodgates and never
be able to close them again. We can't allow terrorism to dic-
tate our foreign policy."

"You're right, Jennifer," sighed President Mendez. "Besides, it's inconceivable to withdraw our troops from the
Middle East. The delicate balance of nations would likely
crumble into a full-blown war."

"So, you're just going to sacrifice our daughter?" said the
first lady, staring at her husband in disbelief.

"No. We'll find another way to get her back." He took her
hand and squeezed it reassuringly. "I promise you."

Colonel Black glanced up at the clock on the wall and
coughed for attention. "Then we've got less than seventy-two
hours to find them."

35

"Connor's in *serious* trouble," said Amir, staring in disbelief at the overhead flat-screen monitor in the Guardian operations room. Colonel Black had forwarded the ransom video via a secure satellite link, and Alpha team had viewed it in shocked silence. Charley, Marc and Ling all wore the same distraught expressions, struggling to come to terms with Connor's dire situation.

"Let's just pray the terrorists don't discover who he *really* is," remarked Bugsy, scrunching up his last packet of chewing gum in frustrated anger and tossing it in the garbage can.

"Why? What difference would that make?" asked Ling.

"He'd become a threat to them," explained their surveillance tutor, his tone grave. "It's rare for a bodyguard to be kidnapped alongside their Principal. They're normally killed right away."

Amir exchanged an uneasy look with Charley.

"Then we had better find them *fast*," said Charley, wheeling herself over to her workstation. "Bugsy, how can we trace the source of the e-mail?"

The tutor pursed his lips thoughtfully. "You can try stripping the header info for the original sender's IP address, then run a reverse DNS lookup," he suggested. "There's a geo-location tool on our system that'll track down the ISP and provide us with a geographical area that the IP is *believed* to be used in."

"You don't seem very certain," remarked Ling as Charley hammered away on her keyboard.

"Such a trail can be easily spoofed," admitted Bugsy. "The IP address might be that of an innocent person or organization who's had it hijacked by the terrorists. And I've no doubt they've used a server relay to bounce the signal around the world."

"You're right," said Charley, slumping back in her chair. "The trail dead-ends at a legitimate book publisher in London."

"Hang on a minute," said Bugsy, hurrying over to his terminal, a sly grin detectable on his lips. "I do have a beta program that might be able to trace the ghost image left behind by the real server. It'll take a bit of time, though."

While Bugsy ran the tracer application, Charley organized the rest of the team.

"Ling, I need you to check the security camera footage around the Jefferson Memorial—before, during and after the ambush. We might pick up some clues—a face or a license plate. Marc, Colonel Black says they found the dead Secret Service agent in an abandoned hangar near Stafford Airport. Execute a digital sweep of the surveillance satellites we have access to and find out if any were over the vicinity at the time. Amir, I'll need your help analyzing the ransom video. Scan its audio track for background noise, accents, anything that might indicate the location of the terrorist's hideout."

Amir sat down at the terminal next to her and logged on. "But won't the Secret Service be doing all of this anyway?" he questioned.

"Of course, but locating Connor and Alicia will be like hunting for a needle in a haystack," replied Charley, expanding the video to full screen and searching for visual leads. "There's every chance they might miss a vital clue. So the more eyes, the better."

36

At least two days had passed . . . or so Connor thought. It was difficult to judge the time, trapped in a windowless cell where the light was never switched off. He and Alicia slept fitfully, a razor edge of fear and uncertainty making it impossible to rest for long. Every so often the door to their cell would be flung open and they'd tense in anticipation of what was to come: *humiliation . . . torture . . . death . . . or possibly freedom?*

But any such thoughts of release were quashed each time the shrouded face of one of their captors appeared. Armed with a gun, he'd bring in a small tray of food: some flatbread, a thin stew and more water, but no cutlery, nothing that could be used as a weapon. Connor would make an attempt at conversation, hoping to find out what was going on. He recalled Colonel Black saying it was important to build a rapport with any hostage-taker—*winning their respect reduces their inclination to hurt their victims.* But their captor wouldn't say anything and wouldn't answer any questions. Just set down the plate and leave. Whether he didn't understand English or ignored Connor on purpose, the lack of information was almost as torturous as their confinement.

A bucket in the corner, replaced infrequently, was their sole means of a toilet. Connor used the mattress as a temporary divider to offer Alicia some privacy at these times. There were no washing facilities provided either, which added to their discomfort, Alicia suffering from that indignity more than Connor.

Early on, Connor had noticed a small camera lens above the door, so they knew they were being watched. And probably overheard too. With that in mind, the two of them had taken the precaution of whispering everything into each other's ears, with their backs to the camera or a hand cupped over their mouths to avoid any possibility of lip-reading.

"Don't you think we should try to escape?" Alicia suggested, looking to the door in the vain hope that one of their guards had forgotten to lock it.

"Only as a last resort," Connor replied, heeding Colonel Black's advice. The chances of success had to be high or the situation so desperate that it demanded an escape attempt. Otherwise such a move was potentially suicidal. Moreover, escape was merely the beginning. The ability to evade the enemy and survive in a foreign country was the *real* challenge. And, since they didn't know where they were, this would be a leap into the unknown. They could be high in the mountains, in a remote hostile village or in the middle of an endless desert.

"Why haven't they found us yet?" Alicia asked, her tone almost pleading.

"Your father's probably still negotiating, while also playing for time."

"But what if that fails? Even I realize the terrorists' terms are impossible to meet. Nobody's worth that sacrifice . . . not even me."

"You mustn't think like that," said Connor, conscious he had to keep Alicia's mind occupied with positive thoughts. Lack of sleep and enforced captivity were making them both overanxious. But she was starting to show signs of self-pity, and he couldn't allow her to drift into despair.

"Listen, when the rescue occurs, drop to the floor immediately," he advised. "There'll probably be a lot of gunfire and smoke from stun grenades. Cover your head with your hands and arms to protect yourself. Let the rescuers know who you are by yelling out your name. And don't make any false moves in case you're mistaken for a terrorist. You don't want to get caught in the cross fire."

Alicia nodded, gazing at him with admiration. "I'm sorry," she whispered.

"For what?" asked Connor.

"For not appreciating you . . ." Alicia seemed to be hunting for the right words. "At the time I was so upset that you weren't who you said you were. Now I'm *glad* you are who you are. My guardian."

She nestled closer to him, seeking the safety of his embrace.

"There's no need to apologize," said Connor.

Alicia buried her head in his chest, and Connor felt his T-shirt moisten with her tears.

"You might be released soon," she said, keeping her voice light and joyous. "That'll be good news."

But Connor sensed the tight knot of terror in her heart at being left to cope on her own.

"I won't leave you," he said.

"But you might not have a choice."

Connor held Alicia close. "I made a promise to your father that I'd protect you, just like my father protected yours. And I will . . . on my life."

37

Malik angrily hurled the remote control at the television in the corner of the sparsely furnished front room. It barely missed, shattering against the wall. On the screen ran a CNN news feed of a blond-haired woman reporting on the aftermath of the bomb attack on Washington, DC. But there was no coverage of the mass pardon for terrorist prisoners that Malik had demanded.

"Why haven't they released any of our brothers yet?" he shouted.

Bahir and Kedar exchanged uneasy glances over their leader's unexpected outburst of rage.

"This is the game they play," Bahir replied softly, putting down the smartphone he'd been tinkering with. "They say 'no negotiation.' But they will. Eventually."

"I wish I had your patience," remarked Malik, shoving a handful of khat leaves into his mouth and chewing manically. "First, the US government tried to stall for time by asking for specific names, which is why I had the list already prepared," he said smugly, tapping a forefinger to his temple. "Then the infidels tried offering us money. A typical American solution to everything, although they didn't have the *respect* to present it to us directly!"

"And now they'll wait until the final hour before contacting us again," Bahir pointed out.

"That's when our brothers will be freed, right?" said Kedar, trying to back up Bahir and reassure their leader.

Malik shook his head, dark thunder swirling in his eyes. "No, I bet they'll plead for an *extension* of the deadline." Fuming at the idea, he spat a green gob onto the floor, just missing Hazim as he entered the room with a tray of food. "But we won't give it to them!"

With a troubled look at his irate uncle, Hazim timidly approached. "Do you still want your dinner?" he asked.

"Of course!" snapped Malik, slumping down on a cushion to eat.

As Malik tore off some flatbread and dipped it into a bowl of hummus, Bahir said, "The Americans' push for delay is understandable, from *their* point of view. They'll be desperate for more time to allow their agencies to pinpoint our location."

"What?" exclaimed Hazim, his hands now trembling as he poured his uncle a cup of coffee. "You mean they could find us here?"

"Don't look so worried, Hazim," Malik said, laughing and

offering a green-stained grin. "They'll *never* find us. Isn't that right, Bahir?"

Bahir nodded confidently. "As I told you before, Hazim, all the jammers are operational and the ghost server relays are fully functional. So we should *all* just try to relax. There are still six hours to go to the deadline."

"But what happens if they don't comply with our demands?" asked Hazim.

Malik unsheathed the *jambiya* from his belt and held the fearsome blade in front of Hazim's face. "Then we prove our *commitment* to our cause."

"Please tell me that's the *last* press conference I have today," said President Mendez, rubbing a hand across his haggard face. "I don't think I can hide my loss much longer."

"Yes, it can be," replied Lara, the press secretary, checking her schedule. "I'll ask the vice president to cover the remaining two."

"Thank you," he sighed. He was worn out, the worry for his daughter leaving a hollow inside so great, he felt paper-thin. With trepidation, he made his way down to the ground floor of the West Wing. So far there'd been no success in locating her, or Connor, and he was beginning to despair. But as he entered the Situation Room, Dirk strode over to him, a victorious gleam in his eye.

"Mr. President, I have some good news. We found them!"

President Mendez was suddenly alert, all tiredness blasted away. "Where?"

"Yemen," replied Karen, calling up a satellite map of the Middle Eastern country on the central monitor. "A private plane flew out of Stafford Airport just two hours after the attacks. The official documentation gave the destination as Riyadh, Saudi Arabia. But a trace of its flight path shows the plane *actually* landing in neighboring Yemen."

"The digital trail also ends there," Dirk said. "There were multiple relay servers and spoofed identities, but the e-mail appears to have originated from the capital city of Sana'a. This was confirmed by Colonel Black's surveillance operative."

Colonel Black now stepped forward. Even though Bugsy had been the first to trace the e-mail, he let this fact pass. There were matters far more important than scoring points against the Secret Service director. "My team also scrubbed the video's audio track and identified a call to prayer sounding in the background." The colonel replayed the short piece of enhanced recording over the Situation Room's speakers, and an echoing chant, barely audible above the hiss and general noise of the video, filled the room. "This particular one is quite distinctive to the region."

President Mendez nodded. "Where exactly do you suspect Alicia is being held?"

"The CIA has eyes on the ground there," explained Karen.

"They report there's been increased activity at a location on the outskirts of the city."

An aerial view of an arid plain and mud-brick city zoomed in on a large building surrounded by a walled compound. The real-time satellite feed revealed four figures patrolling the perimeter.

"I've got a Navy SEAL unit stationed just off the coast of Yemen," announced General Shaw. "They can be at the target within twenty minutes by attack helicopter."

"How certain are you that my daughter's there?" asked President Mendez, studying the aerial shot of the building intently, not daring to let hope enter his heart just yet.

"We can't be one hundred percent sure," admitted Dirk, "but all the indications are strong. An infrared satellite scan indicated people inside, and there were a few suspicious cold spots within the building too."

George interrupted. "Shouldn't we allow time for a negotiated release? We still have five hours left. That's surely our best chance of recovering your daughter unharmed."

"The secretary of state made our position crystal clear on that," Karen reminded them. "The US government cannot be seen to negotiate with terrorists. Besides, there's no guarantee they'll honor their side of a deal anyway."

"More hostages are killed during rescue attempts than from execution by their captors," George noted. "We should wait this out."

"Mr. President, if we don't move now, we may never get another opportunity," urged General Shaw.

President Mendez held up his hand, asking for silence. "What's the mission's probability of success?"

General Shaw swallowed uncomfortably. "I won't lie to you. Intelligence estimates a fifty-fifty chance. But this is our *best* hope of rescuing her."

President Mendez closed his eyes, feeling weighed down by an almost impossible decision—he was literally gambling with his daughter's life.

"The odds are improved by Connor's presence, though," Colonel Black said. "He'll stand by her side and do all that's necessary to protect her."

President Mendez considered this, recalling how his own life had been saved by Connor's father. Opening his eyes, he finally declared, "It's a high-risk strategy, but it's a measure of my desperation. General Shaw, you have my GO for the mission."

38

The two Black Hawk helicopters swooped low over the desert ridges, phantoms against the moonless sky. The six-man Navy SEAL unit, split equally between the two choppers, remained silent and focused, checking their equipment for a final time.

"One minute out," the pilot called through their earpieces.

Lieutenant Webber, "point man" for the operation, clicked off the safety on his assault rifle. Like the other soldiers in his unit, he knew what was at stake and had trained all his life for just such a mission.

In the green glow of his night-vision goggles, the shadowy outline of the compound came into view. He spotted the ghostly face of a sentry peering into the night, hunting for the source of the thudding blades. As they made their final approach, Webber aimed his laser gun sight at the man's head and squeezed the trigger. A split second later the man dropped to the ground, lifeless.

Another sentry appeared and fired his AK-47 blindly in their direction. A crack shot from the other Black Hawk took the man out. The two remaining sentries fled their posts and sprinted for the main building. Webber brought them both down a few feet from the doorway. But he had no doubt the alarm had already been raised. His squad now had little more than a minute to locate and extract the hostages—any longer and it would be too late.

As soon as they'd cleared the compound wall, the SEALs fast-roped from the hovering helicopters to the ground below. Touching down on the hard-packed earth, amid swirls of dust, they unclipped themselves and dashed to the central building. A set of metal double doors served as the entrance, but they'd been locked from the inside.

Kneeling by the doorway, Webber waited a few precious seconds while one of his team, a large man from the Bronx nicknamed Sparky, attached an explosive charge.

"Clear!" barked the soldier, retreating a step and shielding his face.

The device detonated, flinging the metal doors back on their hinges. They banged like temple gongs, the blast echoing around the dusty compound. Inside, the building was cloaked in darkness, but the soldiers' night-vision gear revealed a long empty corridor with doors on either side.

As point man, Webber took the lead.

Suddenly there was an eruption of gunfire. Bullets whizzed past, narrowly missing Webber as he dived into the shelter of a doorway. He and his men returned fire.

"Stairwell!" shouted one of the SEALs.

Webber had line of sight and sprayed the landing with 7.62-caliber rounds. A robed man tumbled down the staircase and landed in a bloody heap on the corridor floor.

A turbaned head then peered out from a room on the far right and immediately disappeared back inside as a hail of bullets raked the corridor wall. Ceasing fire, Sparky hurled a "flashbang" through the open doorway. The stun grenade went off, blinding light and a concussive blast incapacitating the occupant within. Aware they might need the man alive, one of the SEALs cuffed him while the rest of the unit swept the other rooms.

The ground floor was clear; there was no sign of the hostages.

But under the staircase they found an iron gateway and a set of steps leading downward. Dividing into two teams, one SEAL unit headed for the upper floor to subdue any remaining hostiles while Sparky blew the lock on the gate.

Webber descended the narrow stairwell. It was pitch-black, and even his night-vision goggles struggled to pick up anything. As he approached basement level, his ears strained for the sound of footsteps or the telltale *clink* of a round being chambered. He was on the last step when he heard the scrape of a sandal and caught the faintest glint of a blade to his right.

Webber dropped and rolled, squeezing off several rounds at the same time. A man screamed in the darkness. More shots rang out, deafening within the confined quarters of the basement. Sparky and the other SEAL discharged their weapons into the room, neutralizing a second assailant toting an AK-47.

Scrambling to his feet, Webber took no more chances. He tossed flashbangs into the two final chambers. The basement blazed lightning-white, and the air shuddered with the thunderclap of detonating stun grenades. But the SEALs encountered no more hostiles.

Webber noticed a door at the far end of the corridor. He directed Sparky to attach a small charge to the lock. As it exploded, he kicked the door wide open.

"Alicia? Connor?" he called.

Storming in, finger primed on his trigger, Webber was greeted by an empty cell.

39

The door to Alicia and Connor's cell crashed open. The black-robed giant, his face still no more than a pair of raging eyes through the slit of his headscarf, barged in and seized them both by the scruffs of their necks.

"TAHARAK!" he snarled, dragging them through the door.

Connor and Alicia had no choice but to obey as they were shoved along the corridor at gunpoint. Once again they found themselves in the makeshift video room. Two masked terrorists flanked the black flag while the leader stood waiting before the camera, his jeweled dagger in hand.

Connor's heart froze at the sight of the gruesome knife. *The deadline must have passed. The terrorists' demands haven't been met.* He couldn't believe President Mendez had failed to negotiate *at least a delay*. His throat went dry with panic, and he began to hyperventilate. Despite his training, nothing could prepare him for his own execution.

Alicia took his hand, clasping it tightly. Connor met her

terrified gaze, her eyes brimming with tears at the prospect of losing him forever. Connor then felt a strange calm wash over him. Despite the fear for his own life, a cool logic reasoned that if he was sacrificed, *she* could be saved. The US government would be forced to submit to the terrorists' demands, in some form or other, and Alicia would be freed. His death wouldn't be in vain. He'd have protected Alicia with his life, just as he'd promised to.

A ghost of a smile even passed across his lips as he realized he'd be following in his father's footsteps ... right to the very end.

"It'll be all right," he told her as he was pushed toward his fate.

"No, just the girl," ordered the leader. "It'll have more impact."

Connor was stunned by his unexpected reprieve. But his fears quickly turned to Alicia as *she* was forced to kneel before the camera, her back to the ominous flag. Without thinking of the consequences, Connor flung himself at the leader to grab the dagger. But before he'd gone even two steps, the giant hammered a fist into his right kidney. Connor buckled to the floor, wheezing from the blow, pain flaring bright within him.

"Let's send the Americans a message they *can't* ignore," declared the leader, paying no attention to Connor's suffering and gesturing to the man behind the camera.

As the terrorist pressed Record, the leader stood over

Alicia with his knife Alicia became stock-still, her eyes fix-ated on the gleaming steel blade.

"President Mendez," spat the leader to the camera, making no effort to hide his contempt. "We gave you the opportunity to do the honorable thing. To bow to our demands with your head still held high. But you've broken the terms of our deal by attempting—and *failing*—to rescue your daughter. Worse still, you murdered our innocent countrymen in the process. Now we, the Brotherhood of the Rising Crescent, will broad-cast our message to the world—and you will listen and *obey*."

Sheathing his knife, he pulled a gun from his belt and planted the muzzle against Alicia's temple.

Alicia whimpered softly, shying away from the cold hard barrel that promised her death. Yet somehow she managed to overcome her terror and glare up at her captor. "My father will *never* give in to you."

The leader ignored her. "President Mendez, we're men of our word—but it is *you* who have forced our hand."

He pulled the trigger.

"NO!" shouted Connor, reaching out desperately to Alicia as she screamed.

But the gun clicked empty.

The leader stared hard into the camera lens.

"Next time, there *will* be a bullet," he warned. "You've got less than two hours to meet our demands. Do NOT try our patience again!"

40

Charley, Amir, Ling and Marc huddled around the monitor in the operations room, sickened and speechless at the terrorists' ruthless mock execution of Alicia.

"So that's the situation with less than two hours to go," said Colonel Black gravely over the conference video. "This crisis has gone public, the rescue attempt has failed and the president is out of options."

"But where's Connor?" asked Ling. "He wasn't in the video."

Colonel Black's expression darkened. "That I don't know."

"Perhaps he's escaped," Amir suggested, his expression hopeful.

"But we're taught never to leave our Principal," Ling reminded him.

"He could be dead," said Marc flatly.

"NO!" said Charley, denying even the possibility. "We don't know anything, so we cannot presume anything."

"Then why isn't he in the video?" asked Marc.

"The terrorists might be holding him back for the deadline," replied Colonel Black grimly. "I'll contact you if there are any updates."

As the colonel ended his transmission, Alpha team exchanged uneasy looks with one another, each aware of what Colonel Black meant by "deadline."

From the corner of the room came a shout. Leaning back in his chair, Bugsy slapped his forehead with the flat of his hand. "So that's what they've done!" he exclaimed, shaking his head in frustrated disbelief.

"What?" asked Amir.

Bugsy beckoned them over to his workstation. "These terrorists are using a number of crafty technical tricks to mislead us. I've just digitally compared their two videos, and both have a distinctive call to prayer sounding in the background. I extracted them both from the audio. Look at the two wave patterns. They're an exact match!"

On the monitor two graphic sine waves appeared. Using his mouse, Bugsy dragged and dropped one on top of the other. The two patterns were identical.

"So what does that mean?" asked Ling.

"The 'call to prayer' was added in post-production, *after* the recording was made," explained Bugsy. "Whoever their techie is, he's good. He anticipated that we'd search for a location clue in the first video and planted it on purpose for us to discover, making us think they were somewhere else. But he's used the same trick twice."

Bugsy now pulled up a stream of code on his computer workstation.

"Next, I analyzed the two e-mails the president received. As we already know, the terrorists misdirected us over the origin of the e-mail, using fake IP addresses and server relays. I thought my beta program had cracked the source. But see this code here." He pointed to a bewildering collection of numbers and commands. "This indicates that the terrorist programmer set up the equivalent of an 'infinity loop' between servers."

"What's an infinity loop?" asked Marc.

"Like two mirrors opposite each other, this piece of code creates a duplicated signal that bounces between two servers continuously. To my program, this appeared to be a dead end, the 'origin' of the e-mail, whereas in fact it was a 'doorway' that only opens on command."

"So, can you trace the source now?" asked Charley.

Bugsy grimaced and shook his head. "We'd have to access the mirrored servers at the exact moment the terrorists send another e-mail. The chances of doing that are next to zero. I'm afraid there's no more I can do. Wherever he is, Connor's on his own."

41

The cell door clanged shut. Connor kicked at it in frustration and fury.

"You gutless coward! You scumbag!" he roared.

He wanted to pound the terrorist leader to a pulp. He was no longer scared. He was angry.

Anger is only one letter away from danger. His unarmed combat instructor's words repeated in his head. *Control your anger. Otherwise anger will control you and you'll lose focus. As a guardian, you want to fight smarter, not harder.*

Giving the steel door one last kick, Connor checked his temper. He knew he had to think clearly and focus on the situation at hand. But their cruel toying with Alicia's life had boiled his blood. In that split-second moment when the masked leader had pulled the trigger, a crushing grief had overwhelmed him, compounded by the realization that he'd failed to protect her. But no thundering blast of gunfire had followed, and Alicia had opened her eyes, stunned to discover that she was still alive. At first Connor only felt relief. Then he became concerned for her as she just knelt in a zombie-like trance until the end of the video before allowing herself to be dragged back to their cell.

Having vented his fury on the locked door, Connor turned to see Alicia slide down the wall and slump to the floor. She pulled her knees to her chest and stared vacantly at the opposite wall.

"Alicia, are you all right?" he asked.

She didn't reply, just continued gazing into the distance.

Bending down, he touched her shoulder gently, worried the mock execution had broken her spirit. "Alicia? It's okay. I'm with you."

Alicia mumbled something.

"What was that?"

A single tear rolled down her cheek. "We're going to die."

"No, we're not," countered Connor, although his words seemed to ring hollow. With time fast running out, any hopes of rescue were rapidly dwindling. And the terrorists seemed determined to follow through on their threats. If ever there was a situation for a last resort, this was it. They *had* to escape. Connor looked around the tiny windowless cell. He'd already inspected every inch of it for a weakness and had found none. As he racked his brains for a plan, he noticed Alicia trembling from the effects of trauma-induced shock.

"Stay with me," he pleaded, trying to get her to focus on his face. "We'll find a way to escape, somehow. I promise you."

42

"All hell's broken loose," said Lara, the press secretary, dashing in and switching on the TV in the president's private study of the West Wing. "The story's running on every news channel, worldwide."

Turning his gaze to the TV screen, President Mendez sank back into his leather chair and braced himself for the media storm. He was joined in his study by the core members of the National Security Council: the White House chief of staff, the secretary of state, the director of National Intelligence, the director of the Secret Service and General Shaw. Together they watched as a series of news bulletins flashed across the screen.

PRESIDENT'S DAUGHTER TAKEN HOSTAGE!

A clip from the terrorists' video showed Alicia with a gun to her head. Even though he'd already seen it once, President Mendez clenched his fists and shuddered with a combination of cold horror and burning rage. He was one of the most powerful men in the world yet felt utterly powerless to help his own daughter.

The image was replaced with a sound bite of the president addressing a press conference the previous year. *"America stands strong against the threat of terrorism,"* he was saying. *"We don't negotiate with terrorists and never will . . ."*

The news ticker running along the bottom of the screen read, "What will the president do now?"

The segment came to an end, and the monitor filled with scenes of outraged crowds in Times Square calling for Alicia's release. Some people were weeping, others were angry and a growing number were baying for blood.

Finally, the bulletin switched to a view of a dusty compound outside Sana'a. Eight bodies were laid out, surrounded by wailing families. The headline ran, "Attack on farmers' compound— an 'innocent' mistake?"

The newsreel ended with images of spontaneous protests and the burning of American flags in the capital cities of Yemen, Pakistan and Afghanistan.

"Those men *weren't* innocent," growled General Shaw, pounding a fist into his palm. "They were drug dealers. The SEAL unit uncovered a mass shipment of opium in the compound. That's why it was so heavily guarded."

"The Yemeni people won't see it that way," replied Jennifer. The secretary of state stood by the door, her arms crossed, a frown on her face. "And their government is viewing it as an invasion of sovereign territory. We've got a full-blown international crisis on our hands."

"That was always going to be the case," argued Karen. "The question is how did we get it so wrong? I know the surviving gunman admitted that Malik Hussain was behind the drug-running, but the SEAL team found no evidence of Alicia or Connor *ever* having been at that location."

"Listen, we'll have more than enough time for analysis and blame another day," said President Mendez, noticing with dismay that a countdown clock had been posted on the TV news feed. "We have less than fifty-five minutes to meet the midnight deadline. I need to hear your views on what our next move should be. You first, Karen."

"I think we can all agree that these terrorists won't back down. If we don't comply, they'll kill Alicia—or more likely, Connor first to prove their point."

"We don't know that for certain," said Jennifer. "They may bluff again."

"The bombs were no bluff," Karen reminded her.

George held up the list of captured terrorists. "How about we make a concession of a handful of prisoners? The least significant ones. Then we may be able to stall them—even seek a chance of ending this crisis."

"It'll make us look weak," argued General Shaw, taking the side of the secretary of state. "Release any of them and they'll only push for more."

"What about just announcing our troops' withdrawal, then? We don't have to *actually* withdraw from the countries."

Jennifer shook her head. "George, I know you're seeking every possible solution. But such a declaration would send a shock wave through the Middle East. The terrorists know full well that a mere announcement would be enough to create anarchy."

"But if we don't offer the terrorists some consideration at midnight, Connor could die."

"Much as I hate to say this," interjected Dirk, his steel-blue eyes hardening, "it's his duty to make such a sacrifice."

"How can you even *think* such a thing?" exclaimed Karen, shocked by her colleague's coldheartedness.

Dirk shifted awkwardly under her accusing gaze. "Look, if the terrorists kill Connor and we still hold out against their demands, then they've lost. They'll realize that we can't be forced into submission, even when lives are at stake."

"But we're talking here about a child's life," George reminded him. "And how will the world view America then?"

A heavy silence descended on the room, and President Mendez looked to his press secretary for her opinion.

"The fact that Alicia and Connor are still children makes this a highly emotive issue," explained Lara. "The public and media are split on the matter. Half are calling for your daughter's release under *any* circumstances, and the rest think an iron fist should be used. If she is"—Lara hesitated, unable to meet the president's eyes—"killed, there's a danger her blood will be on both the terrorists' and the US government's hands. Whatever decision you make, Mr. President, we must be *seen* to have done everything possible to save her and Connor."

"But we are doing everything possible, aren't we?" asked the president, looking around at his staff.

"Yes," replied Karen quickly, "but I agree with Lara on this—perception is everything."

President Mendez sighed in despair. "Jennifer, what do you advise?"

"You have an impossible choice," Jennifer said. "Give in to their demands and we set a dangerous precedent—one the nation may never recover from. Hold your ground and we maintain the status quo—the Brotherhood may even *lose* crucial support by using such terror tactics. But you risk losing your daughter. This is a no-win situation. You know my views already, but I'm not the one who has to make the ultimate decision on this."

President Mendez studied the secretary of state's ice-maiden face. Despite her seeming lack of compassion, she was an excellent stateswoman, and he knew she only had the good of the nation at heart. His own heart and mind, however, were torn in two. On the one hand, he was the president who'd made an oath to preserve, protect and defend the United States. On the other, he was a father whose whole world was his daughter, and his instinct was to put her first, over everything.

Deep down he knew what *had* to be done. But the choice left a cold spot in his heart, one that would grow like a cancer if either Connor or his daughter died at the terrorists' hands.

The countdown on the TV ticked down to forty-nine minutes.

"Antonio, you may want to see this," interrupted his wife, poking her head around the door.

With the weariness of a burdened man, President Mendez followed her into the Oval Office and over to the bay windows. The first lady drew back the drapes to reveal a view across the South Lawn. In the darkness beyond the iron railings, thousands of flickering flames hovered like fireflies all the way back to the Washington Monument. And even through the thickened bulletproof glass the sound of hymns being sung could be heard like a distant choir of angels. Tears welled up in the president's eyes at the sight of the candlelit vigil in honor of their captive daughter.

"At a time like this, we need all the help we can get," said President Mendez.

"And maybe a little more," suggested the first lady, clasping his hands.

Together they sank to their knees and began praying for a miracle.

43

"At last!" exclaimed Bahir, his eyes widening in delight as he broke through the final safeguard on the firewalled smartphone. The screen burst to life, and a winged shield rotated in 3-D on the retina display. Intrigued by the strange logo, he pressed the home button and the screen filled with icons—*Advanced Mapping, Tracker, Mission Status, Threat Level, SOS* . . .

"What are all those for?" asked Kedar, who sat beside him in the basement room.

"I have no idea," replied Bahir, studying the smartphone with growing consternation. "This phone belongs to that English boy. It survived the EMP blast because of a built-in fail-safe device. The operating system was guarded by an advanced firewall, plus a secondary spyware program that threatened to wipe the contents of the drive every time I attempted to disable it. It even had fingerprint recognition access. But I beat the system in the end." Bahir allowed himself a superior grin.

"Congratulations," said Kedar. "But what does any of that mean?"

Bahir looked at his associate as if he were stupid. "That this phone is no *normal* phone—which means our hostage is by no means normal either."

He pushed Kedar aside to access the computer terminal on his desk.

"What are you doing?" Kedar protested. "We're still waiting for a message from the Americans."

"This could be as important," said Bahir, putting aside the smartphone and launching the computer's Internet browser. He typed "Connor Reeves" into the search engine.

There were too many hits to sift through, so he tightened his parameters by inputting "boy" as well. Most were still irrelevant links. But convinced he was onto something, Bahir searched through "images only." It wasn't until the third page that he recognized Connor's face in a photo. He clicked on the link, opening a website to the *East London Herald* newspaper. The feature was headlined "Local boy Battle of Britain champion!"

Below the caption was a large picture of Connor Reeves holding aloft a silver trophy.

"*Kickboxing champion?*" remarked Bahir. "There's more to

this English boy than meets the eye." He rose from his chair and headed for the door. "Kedar, stay here in case the Americans contact us. I have to go up and speak with Malik."

"Is there a problem?" Kedar asked.

"Possibly. Just keep watch over the hostages."

Kedar nodded and took his place in Bahir's chair. After checking the online mail server for any messages, he heard cries for help over the cell's speaker and glanced up at the video monitor. The English boy was jumping up and down and waving his arms in front of the camera. Kedar was going to ignore his desperate plea for attention when he noticed, in the corner of the cell, the president's daughter having convulsions.

44

At ten minutes to midnight, Malik began honing his *jambiya* for the final time. With feverish intent, he ran the whetstone along the edge of the blade, the scrape of steel and stone sounding like fingernails down a chalkboard.

"So you really intend to *kill* them?" said Hazim, unable to take his eyes off the glinting steel.

Chewing madly on a mouthful of khat, Malik replied, "Just one for starters. Both, if the Americans don't comply."

"We will be condemned by the whole world!" argued Hazim.

"But we will be exalted by our brothers-in-arms!" Malik countered, shooting him an irritable glare. "Now get the coffee I asked for."

Hazim could see by Malik's dilated pupils that he'd chewed too much khat. His uncle was becoming manic and out of touch with reality. "But they're just kids," he reminded him. "Alicia's the same age as my sister."

"She's the offspring of our greatest *enemy*," snarled Malik. He eyed Hazim dubiously. "Don't tell me your belief in our cause is wavering, nephew!"

Hazim shook his head. "No, I don't doubt the cause. But I never thought it would come to this."

As Bahir ran into the room, Malik gave a thin smile. "It was *always* going to come to this."

45

"HELP!" shouted Connor, waving in desperation at the camera lens. "PLEASE! She's having an epileptic fit!"

Behind him, Alicia was thrashing wildly on the mattress. Her eyes were rolled back into her head, only the whites showing. Her breathing was becoming labored, and Connor could hear wet choking gasps like the sound of a dying fish.

He screamed again at the camera, praying that someone was watching or listening. "PLEASE! HELP! She could die!"

Just as he was about to give up hope, the cell door opened.

"Thank goodness," Connor cried as the black-robed giant entered. "She needs a doctor. Right now. The stress of that mock execution must have caused it."

Whether the giant understood him or not, he pushed Connor irritably aside and bent over to examine the writhing girl. As soon as his attention was on Alicia, Connor grabbed the man's head, twisted it and drove it downward.

Taken totally off guard, the terrorist was unable to stop Connor's surprise head-twist attack. His huge mass toppled over. But, rather than guiding the man's head to the ground as he'd been taught in unarmed combat class, Connor used all his strength to smash the terrorist's skull into the concrete floor. The giant grunted and went limp.

Alicia immediately stopped fitting and sat up. "I *really* should be an actress," she said, managing a smile despite the circumstances.

"You can collect your Oscar when we get out of here," Connor replied, taking her hand and pulling her to her feet. His plan had worked perfectly.

As they ran for the open door, Alicia stumbled and let out a cry. Connor turned to see that the terrorist had seized her ankle. Dazed and disoriented as he was, the man, snarling like a pit bull, refused to let go.

If you're forced to fight, end it fast, his combat instructor had said.

Spinning around, Connor kicked the man squarely in the jaw. Teeth flew, and the terrorist lost his grip.

How's that for pain-assisted learning! thought Connor.

But the giant still wouldn't stay down. Spitting blood, he made a desperate lunge for them. Connor shoved Alicia into the corridor as the terrorist bore down on them like a charging bull, his eyes filled with pure rage. Connor threw himself against the cell door. It banged shut, and Alicia turned the key just as the door shuddered under the terrorist's impact.

But mercifully the reinforced lock held.

"What now?" she whispered, glancing nervously along the shadowy corridor.

"*Shh!*" cautioned Connor, putting a finger to his lips and checking the room opposite. It was empty apart from the array of electronic gadgetry and the computer that he'd spotted before. Darting into the room, he wondered if he could send a message. But the keyboard was in Arabic, and besides, he still had no idea where they were. Connor glanced over at a second monitor and saw the giant hurling himself against the cell door, his screams of outrage crackling over the tinny speaker. Connor switched it off. If the other terrorists didn't know about their accomplice's fate, it might give him and Alicia a few more precious seconds to escape. Turning to leave the room, he was astonished to find his smartphone lying on the desk. Grabbing it, he powered it up and pressed his thumb to the fingerprint recognition scanner. The home screen appeared. But any hopes of making an emergency call were quickly shattered. There was no signal.

Alicia touched his arm, urging him to hurry. Connor nodded and shoved the phone into his pocket. Ideally, he'd get reception above ground. Silently beckoning Alicia to follow him, he crept along the corridor toward the stairwell, pausing only to check that the video room was clear. It was deserted.

There were no weapons either—just the ominous black flag and camera on show. Connor steeled himself to climb the darkened stairs, unarmed.

He took it one step at a time, terrified one of the wooden treads would creak under his weight and alert the other terrorists. Alicia stuck close behind, her breathing loud in the darkness. Neither knew what would await them at the top, and Connor feared they'd come face-to-face with someone before they managed to escape the basement. If that happened, they'd have nowhere to run.

But they reached the top of the staircase undetected. A solid wooden door now blocked their route. Connor grasped the handle and slowly turned it. To his relief—and surprise—the door wasn't locked. Pushing it open a fraction, he put his eye to the crack. Beyond was a bright hallway with several rooms leading off from it and what looked like the main entrance door at the far end. He could hear voices. But otherwise the hallway was empty.

Ready? he mouthed to Alicia.

She nodded.

They slipped out and closed the door quietly behind them. Now dangerously exposed, Connor kept Alicia close as they tiptoed along. They were almost to the first doorway, a kitchen coming into view, when a terrorist stepped out.

46

Connor and Alicia found themselves confronted by a young man in his early twenties. No longer in his traditional Middle Eastern robes, the terrorist wore jeans and a blue button-down shirt. He was carrying a pot of steaming coffee on a tray and stood stock-still, shocked by the hostages' unexpected appearance.

For a moment, no one moved.

Then Alicia gasped under her breath. *"Hazim?"*

Suddenly aware he was unmasked, the terrorist cast his eyes to the ground as if deeply ashamed.

"You know him?" Connor whispered in astonishment.

Alicia stared incredulously at the young man before them. "He's one of Kalila's brothers."

Connor now vaguely recalled him collecting Kalila from school on a few occasions. No wonder the Secret Service hadn't picked up on any terrorist surveillance at Montarose School—Hazim would have already been security checked.

Connor realized Hazim must have been responsible for planting the Cell-Finity bug too, when he gave Kalila her new phone and she forwarded the number to Alicia, himself and all her friends. Yet at that precise moment Connor didn't care *who* the terrorist was. His priority was to escape with Alicia.

"Hazim! What's taking you so long?" barked a voice from the far room.

A conflicted look passed across Hazim's face as he glanced from Alicia to the room and back again. He didn't reply, and the man in the room became impatient.

"Bahir, go give him a kick in the backside!"

A man with round steel-rimmed glasses appeared out of a doorway. His eyes widened in shock at seeing their two captives free. "Hazim, don't just stand there!" he cried, dashing into the corridor. "Grab them!"

When Hazim didn't react, Connor seized upon the young man's hesitation. He snatched up the coffeepot and threw the scalding contents into the face of the approaching bespectacled man. The terrorist fell back, screaming, his skin blistering. Connor then one-inch-pushed Hazim in the chest. Hazim flew backward, sprawling onto the kitchen floor. Connor grabbed Alicia's arm and made for the front door.

But they hadn't gone two steps when a bearded man with a hooked nose leaped like a tiger into their path. "Not so fast!" he growled, unsheathing the jeweled dagger from his belt.

Confronted by the formidable blade, Connor recalled his instructor's words: *It's far better to make a good run than a bad stand*. But, with nowhere to run this time, a bad stand was the only option Connor had.

He took the terrorist leader head-on, crescent-kicking the hand that held the dagger. But the leader was deceptively quick. Pulling back, he slashed with the blade. Connor leaped aside, barely avoiding having his stomach sliced open. As the dagger came in for another attack, Connor truly wished he'd worn his stab-proof T-shirt. Pushing Alicia out of range of the knife, he made a lunge forward, seized the man's wrist and twisted it into a jujitsu lock. The leader grimaced in pain, his bones grating, but he refused to let go. The two of them began wrestling for dominance of the knife. They slammed against the wall. The tip of the blade dug into Connor's shoulder. He cried out, losing control of the terrorist's wrist. The leader pinned him to the wall by the throat.

"Who the hell *are* you?" snarled the terrorist leader as Connor choked in his vise-like grip.

Struggling to free himself, Connor spluttered, "Alicia's . . . buddy."

The leader shook his head. "No, you're trouble," he replied, raising his dagger and aiming the sharpened tip at Connor's heart. "Too much trouble to keep alive."

47

For all Connor's protection of Alicia, it was now she who came to *his* rescue. As the dagger arced down, Alicia launched herself at the terrorist leader.

"Leave him alone!" she cried, landing on his back.

Clinging on for all she was worth, she clawed at his face with her long fingernails, gouging at both his eyes. The leader roared in fury and pain. Releasing Connor, he snatched at the wildcat on his back. He grabbed hold of an arm and flung her off. Alicia flew through the air, struck the opposite wall and landed in a dazed heap, blood trickling from a gash on her forehead.

Seized by bloodlust, the leader turned on her. Deep red score-marks lined his face, and one eye was a bloody pulp.

"You'll pay for that," he yelled, brandishing his dagger. "I'll cut *your* face to pieces!"

"NO! UNCLE MALIK, DON'T!" Hazim shouted as he ran

from the kitchen and stepped between them. "She's just a girl."

"She's an infidel," spat the terrorist leader, glaring at his nephew through his one good eye. "Now out of my way or I'll go through you to her."

Connor could see Hazim was trembling with fear, but he held his ground.

Malik appeared to back down. Then with the speed of a striking cobra, he drove the dagger into Hazim's gut. Hazim gasped in shock, his eyes bulging, his whole body shuddering.

"I've always questioned whether you had the *stomach* for this mission," Malik said, smirking as he drove the blade up to the jeweled hilt and twisted. Hazim screamed, his blood now spilling onto the floor.

Connor seized his moment and rushed over to Alicia. She was still stunned from the blow against the wall. Ignoring the pain in his shoulder, he half carried her into the kitchen, praying they'd find a back door.

"Bahir, get after them! And where the hell's Kedar?" Malik shouted from the hallway. "They're escaping!"

Connor's gamble paid off. On the other side of the kitchen was an exit leading to a wooden veranda. Flinging open the door, Connor and Alicia staggered out into a large garden bordered by a high brick wall. A shimmer of moonlight revealed a small shed next to the wall and the silhouettes of tall trees beyond.

"This way," he said as the fresh air brought Alicia back to her senses and she found her feet again.

They fled into a warm starlit night, the darkness quickly enveloping them. From the kitchen, Malik's voice barked, "Get the guns! Search the garden."

Feet thundered onto the wooden veranda just as Connor and Alicia reached the shed.

"Which way did they go?" said a voice, urgent and angry.

Connor noticed a woodpile stacked beside the shed. Gritting his teeth against the burning fire in his shoulder, he pushed Alicia up. He could feel that his shirt had become slick with his own blood. They clambered onto the shed's roof, from where they could just reach the top of the garden wall.

"Over there!" came a shout.

Connor was caught in the beam of a flashlight. There was a gunshot, and a bullet ricocheted inches from his head. He and Alicia flung themselves over the wall, hung on to the tile-capped lip, then dropped down to the other side. The distance was farther than either of them had anticipated, and they both crumpled to the rocky ground. Alicia let out a cry.

"I've . . . twisted my ankle," she grimaced, clasping her foot.

That was the last thing they needed. But Connor wasn't going to fail in his duty now. He put an arm under Alicia's shoulder and hauled her to her feet. There was a slim chance the trees might conceal their escape. Hurrying as fast as her ankle and the terrain would allow, they beat a path through the undergrowth and weaved between the trees.

As they fled, Connor pulled his phone from his pocket. Still no signal.

Then he noticed *Insert SIM Card* flashing at the bottom of the screen.

Cursing, Connor was about to discard the phone when his finger jogged the screen and Amir's SOS app appeared. In his rush to escape, he'd forgotten all about it. Connor launched the app and pressed Send.

He just hoped the phone had enough battery life to do the job.

48

In the operations room of Guardian headquarters, the atmosphere was tense and agitated. Charley drummed her fingers on the arm of her wheelchair. Marc sat with his head in his hands. Next to him, Ling rubbed her eyes with exhaustion and took another sip of an energy drink. Amir was pacing nervously up and down, while Bugsy stared blankly at the monitor of his terminal, defeated by the server source code.

"The deadline's past," said Amir, glancing up at the clock. "Why haven't we heard anything yet?"

"No news is good news," offered Bugsy.

"But the terrorists were pretty insistent on their deadline," said Ling.

"Maybe the president struck a deal with them?" Marc suggested.

Charley shook her head sorrowfully. "We'd have heard from Colonel Black by now."

They all lapsed back into anxious silence. Charley began

to bite her nails. She felt partly responsible for Connor's fate. She was the operations leader, after all. An ominous thought passed through her mind. *Perhaps bad karma's following me since my last assignment as an active guardian.* Nothing, it seemed, had gone right for her since that fateful day. Connor had been a turning point in her life, or so she had hoped. But now it appeared he would be yet another dead end. Literally.

A computer terminal began beeping incessantly.

"What's that?" asked Ling.

Charley looked over at Amir, and they blurted out simultaneously, "SOS!"

Rushing to the terminal, Amir woke the monitor and his jaw dropped in disbelief.

"If this really *is* Connor, then you're not going to believe where they are . . ."

Charley sped over and stared at the screen in equal astonishment.

"Amir, relay the coordinates to Colonel Black, right now!"

49

Connor and Alicia rushed headlong through the under-growth, branches and bushes tearing at their faces and clothes. The forest was inky black, the moonlight struggling to penetrate the canopy above, and Connor could only haz-ard a guess at the direction they were headed. But as long as it was away from the terrorists, he didn't care. Behind them, he could hear the men crashing through the bushes in hot pursuit. Alicia struggled valiantly, but with her injured an-kle, the terrorists were gaining on them fast. Glancing back, Connor could see the lights of the terrorists' flashlights sweeping the area for them.

"Leave me," she panted, leaning against a tree trunk to catch her breath. "Go and get help."

"No," said Connor. "A guardian *never* leaves their Principal. Nor does a friend."

She managed a weak smile. "You're one hard date to get rid of!"

Bearing more of her weight, Connor pressed on despite his own injury. Alicia bit down on her lip as pain rocketed up her leg with every step. The shouts of the terrorists grew louder. Several bullets whizzed past, shearing off chunks of bark and sending splinters into their path. Hobbling down a slope, Connor and Alicia burst from the undergrowth and hit an asphalt road. A car zoomed by, horn blaring as it almost ran them over.

"STOP!" cried Connor, trying to flag the vehicle down.

But the red taillights disappeared rapidly into the distance.

"Did you see that?" asked Alicia, her eyes wide.

"What?"

"The license plate!"

"No, but keep moving," Connor insisted, trying to hurry Alicia across the road before the terrorists appeared. But she continued to stare after the car. Then he too was brought to a sudden halt by a road sign . . . in English:

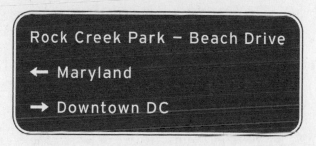

"Rock Creek Park?" said Alicia, reading the sign twice and still doubting her eyes. "We're *still* in Washington!"

Connor couldn't believe it either. The disorientation of

their captivity, the terrorists' robes, the constant use of Arabic and the traditional style of food had all convinced him that they were being held in the Middle East. As the truth dawned on him, Connor tried to recall the park's layout from his briefing notes. He knew it wasn't a particularly wide park, a couple of miles at the most, so they'd soon come to the city suburbs. They just needed to keep off the road and out of sight until they could reach help.

The sign clanged, loud and harsh, as a bullet pierced a hole dead center through the first *"o"* of *Downtown*. Connor spun around to see Malik and his men scrambling down the slope, guns leveled at them.

"Stay right where you are!" warned Malik.

Instinctively protecting Alicia, Connor propelled her toward the bushes on the other side of the road. Gunfire ripped through the night, bullets peppering the road at their feet. They dived for the cover of the trees, landing hard on the rocky ground. As they scrambled back up, Alicia's ankle finally gave way beneath her and she screamed.

"Come on!" cried Connor, his adrenaline driving him on as he lifted her onto his shoulders and ran.

But in those fateful few seconds the terrorists had caught up, and Connor found himself confronted by the barrel of Malik's gun.

"Make one false move and I'll put a bullet through both

of you," said Malik, his eye still bloody from where Alicia had clawed him.

Gently lowering Alicia to the ground, Connor stood in front of her—his body, her shield.

"I admire your commitment to the girl," Malik said, smirking to reveal a row of yellowed teeth. "A *boy* willing to make the ultimate sacrifice . . . and so you will."

The gunshot rang through the forest.

50

"Will he live?"

"Unfortunately, it appears so," replied Kyle as he eyed the wounded terrorist with contempt.

Malik lay handcuffed to a stretcher, a drip in his arm, a mass of bloody bandages wrapped around his chest. Two medics were checking his vital signs and preparing to transfer him into the waiting ambulance.

Connor sat on the back step of a second ambulance, a medic stitching up the knife wound to his shoulder. He could feel the tug of the stitching against his flesh, but the anesthetic was keeping the pain at bay.

When Connor had been confronted at point-blank range with Malik's gun, he'd thought his life was over. He'd braced himself to take the bullet for Alicia. A final and fatal act of protection. And the only thing, as a bodyguard, he had left to give. But it was Malik who fell to the ground, screaming.

Immediately after the gunshot, the forest had erupted

with Secret Service agents. Connor had thrown himself on top of Alicia as there was a furious exchange of gunfire. One terrorist was instantly shot down. The others were subdued in a matter of seconds. Then Connor and Alicia were encircled by an impenetrable barrier of agents, Kyle among them.

"That'll be some battle scar," Kyle remarked, nodding at Connor's wound when the medic had finished.

Connor smiled; he supposed it would look kind of cool. A badge of honor to show Charley, Amir and the others when he got back to the United Kingdom.

As the surviving terrorists were bundled, hands bound, into a windowless armored van, the director of the Secret Service strode over to Connor.

"How many did you say there were?" asked Dirk.

"Six, that I saw."

"Well, we've accounted for five," the director said, frowning.

Connor looked toward the armored van. "I don't see the one with glasses."

"The one you scalded with coffee?" Dirk asked. Connor nodded, and the director immediately got on his radio, circulating the man's description to his team. He turned back to Connor. "I have two units sweeping the park. With any luck, they should apprehend him. We've also checked out the house and found the terrorist you locked up. There was a dead one in the hall too. Did you do that?"

Connor shook his head. "That was the leader's work."

Dirk raised an inquiring eyebrow.

Connor thought of Kalila. She'd be devastated by the news of her brother's treachery—unless he could offer her some comfort through his last-minute act of redemption. "The guy was Hazim, a brother of one of Alicia's classmates. He had a change of heart and tried to save us."

Dirk nodded and instructed Kyle to make a note of it.

"What's going to happen to the terrorist leader?" asked Connor as the doors to Malik's ambulance were slammed shut and he was driven away, sirens blaring.

"He'll first be taken to a secure medical facility for questioning, then charged with kidnapping, terrorism and murder," replied Dirk. "He'll no doubt spend the rest of his life in a maximum-security prison, although he deserves much worse."

Connor looked over his shoulder into the back of his ambulance. Alicia was laid out on a stretcher, her ankle bound. A medic was tending to the laceration on her forehead, and a drip had been inserted into her arm to treat for mild dehydration and shock.

The director noted his concern. "Don't worry, the medic says she'll be fine . . . all thanks to the great job you've done in protecting her."

Connor looked up at Dirk, dumbfounded by his uncharacteristic praise.

Dirk unpinned the small Secret Service badge on the lapel

of his jacket and fastened it to Connor's top. The five-pointed star glimmered in the ambulance's twirling red and white lights.

With a rare smile, he declared, "You've earned this, Agent Reeves."

51

July 4

"Today is Independence Day!" declared President Mendez, standing before the microphone on the steps of the Lincoln Memorial. "Not only for the United States, but for my daughter, Alicia."

Connor could barely hear himself think as the crowd roared its delight. Bathed in glorious July sunshine, thousands upon thousands of people had gathered to celebrate Alicia's freedom. American flags and pennants were being waved in joyous triumph, a rippling sea of red, white and blue that encircled the Reflecting Pool and stretched as far as the eye could see. Connor thought this was what it must have been like for Dr. Martin Luther King Jr. as he delivered his famous "I Have a Dream" speech.

"I prayed for a miracle," proclaimed the president as the crowd quieted down. "And one was delivered."

He glanced over his shoulder at his daughter. Just offstage stood Connor in a cream-colored shirt, baseball cap and mirrored shades. For a brief moment the president looked directly at him, his eternal gratitude apparent.

"But I haven't only God to thank for that," continued President Mendez, addressing the crowd. "There are certain people who work tirelessly and endlessly to protect me and my family. And they're the ones responsible for the safe return of my precious daughter. I'm forever grateful to the Secret Service and all the security agencies. I must also thank *you*, the American people, for your support in my family's darkest hour."

There was a wave of heartfelt applause.

Connor knew he wouldn't be thanked publicly. Nor would his role in the operation ever be admitted, since the Guardian organization had to remain covert to be effective. It had been agreed that the Secret Service would receive all the credit for Alicia's rescue. However, Connor didn't feel cheated. In fact, he had no desire for any such acknowledgment. Just seeing Alicia alive, free and happy was enough for him. He now understood why his father had been so compelled to be a bodyguard. The reward was in the knowledge that a life had been protected and saved. And each day after that was a gift.

"Terrorism will *never* defeat America!" President Mendez thumped the podium. "However low they sink, we will never bow to their pressure. For we are a nation of strength, of determination and of love. We are *one* family."

He beckoned to his wife and daughter to join him in front of the cheering crowd. Alicia glanced at Connor, a beaming smile on her lips meant only for him. Connor returned the smile. They hadn't had much chance to talk since their escape, Alicia being reunited with her family and Connor being debriefed by both Colonel Black and the Secret Service. But he knew there was still a great deal to be said between them. And once things settled down, he hoped for just such an opportunity.

Caught up in the emotion of the event, Connor felt the urge to take a photo. It was a unique moment, and he wanted to share it with his friends back at Guardian headquarters. Slipping his phone out of his pocket, he snapped a picture of Alicia approaching the podium and the flag-waving crowd beyond.

Immediately after he took his finger off the button, an icon on the screen began to flash red. Connor thought the battery was dying, but then the face-recognition software app launched, and a series of thumbnail photos appeared. The first was of him and Alicia on the steps of the Lincoln Memorial, another was at Montarose School before entering the school dance and the third was the one he'd just taken. Each photo zoomed in on a red-highlighted face in the background.

Connor felt a cold sense of dread as he too recognized the face.

52

Once is happenstance. Twice is circumstance. Three times means enemy action.

Connor's alert level shot up to Code Orange. He searched the crowd, his eyes scanning the countless faces among the forest of flags and pennants. Quickly referring to his phone for a position, he found the person he was looking for.

With a large bent nose and hound-dog eyes, the man was instantly recognizable. He'd been the face behind the glass, the thirsty worker at the water fountain and, in all likelihood, the mysterious figure in the corridor at the school dance. On this day, the groundskeeper from Montarose School was just a spectator. But he appeared agitated and, despite the hot day, was oddly dressed in a bulky sports jacket.

Connor pressed his earpiece.

"Bandit to Bravo One. Suspect spotted two o'clock of the podium."

"Bravo One to Bandit. Describe," came back Kyle's voice immediately.

"Tall, black hair, large nose, wearing red sports jacket, brown T-shirt with—"

As Connor relayed his description, the groundskeeper reached into his jacket.

Time suddenly seemed to slow down for Connor. The first thing he thought he saw was the butt of a gun protruding from the man's hand. Connor waited a beat, not wishing to "cry wolf" again and ruin another celebration. Then a barrel emerged from the jacket and there was no longer any doubt. His mind switched to Code Red.

"GUN!" he barked into his mic.

A fraction of a second later, another agent spotted the threat. But the groundskeeper was already bringing his weapon around on Alicia. She was oblivious, her gaze directed toward her father. And so were the people in the crowd, who were entirely focused on the first family. Only the Secret Service agents were paying the man any attention. As two agents rushed to tackle the assassin, Connor launched himself toward Alicia. Each step felt like he was running through thick mud, the distance between them stretching rather than closing.

Agents from the president's protective detail were also moving in to secure President Mendez and his family.

Connor reached Alicia just as he heard two gunshots. He drove his hip into her, and "the Shove" knocked her sideways. He was about to follow and provide body cover when the bullets hit him with the force of a battering ram.

53

Malik's eyes flickered open, and a windowless gray room swam into view. The harsh neon strip light on the ceiling hurt his one uncovered eye; the other was blessedly shaded by a bandage. Next to his bed was an ECG monitor, softly beeping at a regular pulse. An IV drip hung beside it, the tube attached to a cannula in his left arm. Malik felt maddeningly thirsty, and his lungs whistled with every shallow breath he took. He tried to sit up, but it was as if a lead weight had been dropped on his chest. Glancing down, he saw that his torso was swathed in bandages, a patch of blood seeping through. Turning his head slowly, he became aware of a man in a white coat sitting at the end of his bed.

"Who . . . are . . . you?" wheezed Malik.

"I have some questions," said the man.

"Talk . . . to my lawyer."

The man ignored his suggestion and took a smartphone

from his pocket. "You were paid ten million dollars in advance for kidnapping the president's daughter."

Malik went still. "How do you know that?"

"The people I represent paid you that amount. And they want it back for *failure* to fulfill the terms of the deal."

Malik felt a chill run down his spine. "B-but I succeeded. That English boy, Connor Reeves, is to blame."

The man appeared unmoved by his argument. Clutching at the possibility of a deal, Malik said, "What would I get in return?"

"We can talk about your release afterward. First, I need your account details and transfer code," said the man, tapping at the screen of his smartphone.

Malik considered the offer for a brief moment only. If the central cell was powerful enough to reach inside the US government, then it was powerful enough to free him. Malik recited the digits from memory. The man typed the account number and code into his smartphone. Once the transaction was complete, he returned his attention to Malik.

"Now everything is in balance. Equilibrium, you might say. We can proceed. What does the Brotherhood know about the funding of your operation?"

"Nothing," replied Malik. "I never told anyone about the central cell."

The faintest trace of a smile passed across the man's face.

"Excellent." He put his hand into his coat pocket and pulled out a large fountain pen. "So you're the only link."

The man removed the nib to reveal a long syringe.

"What are you doing?" spluttered Malik, his uncovered eye widening in horror at the sight of the needle. "You're not a doctor!"

"No," the man replied, calmly inserting the syringe into the Y-connector of Malik's IV drip. "I'm your executioner."

"But I won't talk," promised Malik, sweat suddenly breaking out on his brow. "I don't even know who you are!"

The man depressed the plunger on his pen, and a clear liquid fed into the drip. A second later, Malik felt a fire ignite in his arm, as if molten iron were coursing through his veins. He tried to scream, but the sheer agony of the poison spreading through his body took all his breath away. Arching his back and writhing, he clawed at the man in a desperate attempt to stop him. The man watched, impassive to his suffering. Then the poison reached Malik's heart and he slumped, lifeless, onto his bed, the ECG beep turning to a continuous drone.

"And you never *will* talk," said the man, putting the nib back on his pen and leaving the room.

54

"How's the leg?" inquired Colonel Black, standing beside Connor's bed in the secure wing of George Washington University Hospital.

Connor shifted uncomfortably. He felt as if he'd been run over by a bus, and his thigh still throbbed like wildfire. "Better," he replied, wincing, his badly bruised ribs making it difficult to breathe.

His life had only been saved by his decision earlier that morning to wear his bulletproof shirt. The first round had hit him dead center in the chest, resulting in blunt trauma—excruciating but survivable. The second bullet had struck his unprotected thigh and he'd dropped to the ground, blood pouring from the wound over the white marble steps. Connor had initially felt nothing, the burst of adrenaline masking the pain. And in those few moments of shocked numbness, he'd watched the groundskeeper being tackled by the two agents and finally disarmed. Alicia had screamed his name as she was evacuated away by the Secret Service. But only when she was out of the danger zone did Connor relax, and then a whiteout of pain exploded in his leg. Everything after that was a blur of agents, rapid-response medics, ambulances and nurses.

"Excellent," said Colonel Black, with an approving nod at Connor's brave response. "Your doctor tells me it's just a flesh wound, so you'll be back on your feet in no time."

He handed Connor a get-well card.

"You shouldn't have!" jested Connor, surprised by the colonel's thoughtfulness.

"I didn't," he replied, straight-faced. "It's from Alpha team."

Connor smiled. He supposed it was a bit much to expect sympathy from a battle-hardened former soldier of the Special Air Service, a unit of the British Special Forces. He opened the card, and his smile widened into a grin when he read the message: *To the bullet-catcher!*

"Charley's due in tomorrow," revealed the colonel.

Connor looked up. "She's coming *here*?"

Colonel Black raised an eyebrow. "I have to return to HQ, and she volunteered."

Connor was delighted by this news. It would be good to have a friend around, especially one who'd understand a little of what he'd been through. The US government had been quick to suppress media reporting of his true role in protecting the first daughter. He was just a casualty of the "crazed gunman," and because of the baseball hat and sunglasses he'd been wearing, his identity hadn't been revealed. Even his name had been changed on the hospital records. His own mother and gran didn't know the whole story either. They'd been told he was involved in a mountain-biking accident while on his student exchange program. The colonel had arranged a video call to reassure them. And although Connor didn't like keeping his family in the dark, he appreciated the need to do so—just like his father had when working for the SAS.

Connor put aside the card. "So what's the news on the groundskeeper? Was he connected to the terrorists?"

Colonel Black shook his head. "No, it doesn't appear so. The Secret Service intercepted the missing terrorist yesterday, a man called Bahir, as he was trying to escape to Mexico under a false passport. The groundskeeper appears to be a lone wolf. They checked Alicia's school locker on your suggestion and found a note threatening to kill her for 'ignoring him.' It seems he had some type of obsession with her."

Connor shuddered at the thought. If it hadn't been for the water pistol incident at the school dance, the Secret Service might have followed up on his original call-in about the locker. But at least all the terrorists had been captured—that was reassuring news for both him and Alicia.

"Tell me, did the Secret Service find out any more about that double agent?"

"Dead end," replied the colonel. "Agent Brooke's apartment burned down a few days back. The FBI is investigating. But there's no need to concern yourself with that. Remember, you're a bodyguard, not a spy. Speaking of which . . ."

Colonel Black reached into his jacket pocket and pulled out a winged Guardian shield.

"For outstanding bravery in the line of duty," he declared, pinning the badge to Connor's chest and saluting him.

Connor glanced down and saw that the winged badge was *gold*.

55

"I was right to trust my daughter to a Reeves guardian," said President Mendez, making his personal farewell in the Blue Room of the White House Residence, along with his wife and Alicia. "You're most certainly your father's son. You've proven beyond doubt that you have his courage, dedication and strength of character."

Connor smiled gratefully at the president's words. The bruising on his chest had disappeared, and his leg, although stiff, was almost fully healed. But now another wound was beginning to heal too—the one in his heart caused by his father's death. Being compared to his father was as close as Connor could get to actually *being* with him again. And that meant a great deal.

"I just did my duty, Mr. President," replied Connor.

"You went way beyond the call of duty," said the first lady, kissing him on the cheek and embracing him. "There are no words to express how thankful we are for your protecting our treasured daughter."

"This gift may go some way toward helping you in the future," said President Mendez, handing Connor a dark blue passport. "In recognition of your services, I've granted you honorary citizenship of the United States. With this, you'll be able to call on any of our government's resources and gain consular protection from our embassies throughout the world."

"Thank you, Mr. President," replied Connor, accepting the unique and powerful gift.

President Mendez and his wife stepped aside to allow their daughter to come forward. Wearing a lilac summer dress, her long locks pinned back and a touch of makeup highlighting her natural beauty, Alicia was a far cry from the distraught and terrified hostage she had been the previous month.

"We'll leave you two together," said the president tactfully as he led the first lady out onto the South Portico.

Alicia waited until the doors closed behind them, then turned to Connor. "I suppose this is really good-bye," she said, biting her lip and blinking back tears.

Connor nodded. He hadn't been looking forward to this moment either. They'd been through so much together, and shared a close, seemingly unbreakable bond. It felt wrong to part like this. But now that Alicia understood the necessity of Secret Service protection, Kyle and his team could function 100 percent effectively and Connor's role was no longer required.

"Thank you for protecting me," said Alicia. "Without you, I could never have survived being a hostage."

"Without *you*, I wouldn't have survived either," admitted Connor.

Alicia gave him an affectionate smile. "Well, you'll be pleased to know I've accepted my role as the first daughter. I appreciate that although it offers me many unique opportunities, my freedom is limited—and for good reason. I won't be running away from the Secret Service again!"

Smiling ruefully, she glanced in Kyle's direction. Kyle nodded before discreetly leaving the room. Now that they were truly alone, Alicia took a step toward Connor. She studied his face, seemingly trying to commit it to her memory.

"I know you can't stay . . . ," she whispered, "but this is to remember me by."

Alicia wrapped her arms around his neck and kissed him. Connor's breath was taken away, and he became lost in the moment.

Suddenly the door to the room opened.

Alicia broke away. "Kyle, I asked not to be disturbed—"

"Sorry, I didn't get the message," replied Charley, wheeling herself in. She glanced at Connor, who was guiltily rubbing away a faint smear of lipstick with the back of his hand.

"Our car's here," she said pointedly.

Connor nodded, unable to meet her questioning stare.

"*Already?*" said Alicia.

"We have a plane to catch," Charley replied, breezily pivoting on the spot and heading for the door.

While Charley's back was turned, Connor took Alicia's hand and looked her in the eyes. "I definitely won't forget you . . . or that kiss," he promised.

Then, with great reluctance, he hurried after Charley. At the threshold to the room, he glanced back. Alicia stood silhouetted by the window, gazing out across the South Lawn.

"Don't worry, Connor, I'll protect her," said Kyle, who stood sentry at the door.

Knowing she was in safe hands, Connor headed through the White House's main entrance hall and out to the driveway of the North Portico. Charley was already waiting for him in the car.

"Honestly, I didn't make the first move," he explained, offering a sheepish grin as he clambered in next to her. "Besides, I'm no longer *officially* protecting her—"

"It's not important," said Charley, although Connor could tell she was annoyed.

"Surely you must've found yourself in similar situations," he pressed.

Charley gave him a look that he couldn't quite read. Then her expression softened. "Don't worry, I won't tell the colonel."

With that she placed a black folder on Connor's lap. The folder was marked Confidential in red lettering and had a silver winged shield embossed on the cover.

"Your next assignment."

Connor stared at Charley in disbelief. "But I just got out of the hospital! Besides, who says I still want to be a bodyguard?"

"The colonel," she replied, handing him a scratched key fob. "He says it's in your blood . . . and he's never wrong."

As they drove away from the White House, his Principal safe and secure, Connor studied the key fob. His father's face stared back at him, and Connor thought he could discern the ghost of a proud smile.

Connor couldn't deny the facts. It *was* in his blood. He was born to be a bodyguard.

The End

The Next Pulse-Pounding Mission

Is Available in Bookstores Now!

Turn the Page for a Sneak Peek at

Book 3: Hijack

"Keep your head down!" Connor shouted as a barrage of bullets raked the brick wall.

His Principal had gone into shock and kept trying to bolt from their hiding place. But that was the worst possible reaction the boy could have. A casual stroll down the street had turned into a bodyguard's nightmare, and now they were pinned down in a well-planned ambush.

Connor knew his next move would be crucial. In his head, he ran through the A-C-E procedure . . .

Assess the threat. Two shooters. One in an alley. Another behind a tree. Intention to kill, not capture.

Counter the danger. His first priority was to find cover and secure the Principal. But the low brick wall they had hidden behind provided only temporary protection. As soon as the shooters repositioned themselves, he and his Principal would be exposed again.